The Dragon Stone Conspiracy

A STROWLERS NOVEL BY

Amanda Cherry

ZOMBIE ORPHEUS ENTERTAINMENT

SEATTLE, WA

Funded on Kickstarter by 612 passionate *Strowlers* fans.

Zombie Orpheus Entertainment
4152 Meridian St #105-65
Bellingham, WA 98226
www.zombieorpheus.com

Pepper Elizabeth Jones is portrayed on screen by Lisa Coronado.

Cover layout and design by Ben Dobyns and Gabriel Gonda.
Cover photography by Dawndra Budd.
Editing and interior design by Ben Dobyns.
German language editing by Poisonpainter.

The Dragon Stone Conspiracy/Amanda Cherry. -- 1st ed.
ISBN 978-1-944217-29-7

For Marilyn and all those who march beside her.

Thank you for standing against fascism
wherever it may be found.

You wind your way to the center... and when you're in the middle you have a chance. To change, to grow, or to die.

—JOSIAH, STROWLER

Prologue

I t was a rare gathering of friends and enemies, many who had assiduously avoided each other for decades—a few for centuries and then some.

But one didn't refuse Vadoma without consequences, especially if one had ever accepted sustenance or refuge in her home. Born a mortal into an infamously powerful Romani clan, she'd found her way into the Changing Lands as a curious child and had scarcely set foot back into the ordinary since. She'd learned to straddle the realms in a singular fashion, appearing out of nowhere to help, or to hinder, a weary traveler according to her whims.

These days her powers rivaled that of any native Fäe, and what's more—she knew it.

Any obligation to a Fäe was as binding as a legal contract,

with far more dire consequences than those for most mortal transgressions. An invitation from Vadoma was not a request. Even the most powerful were granted no exemption.

So they had come. From all corners of the globe they'd arrived: the churlish Grey Man in fishmonger's weeds, whittling as though unengaged but undoubtedly keenly aware of every going-on; the singer Holde Berge, her too-prominent cheekbones slathered in rouge and her tall, stocky form sheathed in a sequin gown almost too gaudy to be true; and holding court over them all, sardonic and smoking in the corner, The General.

The General. *The Righ*. McCaslin to those who dared use her given name. Terrible and ancient, she was more powerful than all the rest combined, save for the fact of her captivity. But it was this fact, and this fact alone that made her accessible…approachable…amenable to their company. One of her kind ranging free would never have considered such a meeting. Her presence was mission critical but terrifying all the same. The others gave her as wide a berth as their surroundings would allow.

They were gathered in her chamber, of course. If you wanted an audience with the Righ, you had to come to her. None among them had relished entering into the General's sanctum, but all involved took the venue as an indication of the seriousness of what Vadoma had to tell them.

It was helpful that the underground den was as close to

neutral ground as existed among them, made more appealing by the fact The General couldn't follow them if a hasty escape became necessary. Each knew from experience that one flare of her legendary temper would be more than enough to necessitate retreat.

After all, they had—to a person—helped imprison her here centuries ago. It had taken Merlin themself to make it so. Now the Righ existed out of time, anyplace and no place, feeding on the trauma of mortals as doors to her cell opened and closed into and out of mankind's greatest tragedies; the portals appearing all on their own and completely out of the General's control. That was Merlin's magic, too, and the Righ had made no secret of her frustration with present circumstances.

The General's kind was known to hold grudges. It was likely for this reason Vadoma had wasted no time getting to her point.

"There is a new Guardian," she announced, scarcely a moment after the last of her guests arrived. She scanned the room then, her face taking on the kind of gentle smile that always fooled humans into believing she cared about their individual fates; the same way rats in a maze might believe the scraps from their masters were given in love. No one present was falling for it.

"Nonsense," Holde Berge replied, shaking her red-dyed locks in disgust, her artificial eyelashes batting insistently.

"Only three of five remain."

"Four," the Grey Man whispered, his hands never ceasing work on the fish emerging from the ash wood between his left thumb and forefinger.

"The actress doesn't count. She's a dilettante. A fool." Holde Berge didn't bother to contain her disgust.

"Selfishness and foolishness are potent when combined with enough power," replied the Grey Man. He set down his whittling to look the singer in the eye.

"Enough about Trudy Lane," the singer spat, "she's a talentless hack and we all know it."

The General chuckled under her breath. How long had it been since she'd had this kind of entertainment? Petty squabbles of lesser beings had always been a joy to behold. And what did she care for the fate of the Guardians, anyway?

Vadoma raised her hand and the room quieted instantly. "The fifth talisman, long lost, has passed into dangerous hands."

"Dangerous, how?" the General asked, suddenly engaged, her thick Irish brogue drawn out as though the words came in slow motion.

"The kind that would seek to fully undo us," Vadoma replied. "a True Believer."

"In magic?" the Grey Man inquired, but he did not look up.

"In truth and justice. She wants to build a better world for humanity."

The Fae exchanged somber glances then. Dilletantes were one thing. *Activists* were another. And it sounded as though this potential Guardian was one of the latter. That was not to be taken lightly.

They remembered all too well the first Guardians, the persecutors and jailers who had destroyed the old world of magic in the name of progress, science, and enlightenment. Breaking even an ounce of their overwhelming, enraging power had been the work of a hundred-and-thirty years, patiently executed across the decades, beyond the span of individual human lives or memory.

Vadoma continued. "If the remaining Guardians find and recruit her, we could be set back another half century."

The General snorted delicately from her perch in the corner, a wisp of smoke curling from her nostril.

"Is there something you wish to say, your highness?" Vadoma asked, an eyebrow arched in perfect mimicry of grandmotherly concern.

The General folded her hands in her lap and sighed. "Airplanes are due to strike the Twin Towers in fifty-eight years tonight," she answered. "I can feel the portal stirring just beyond my reach. It will open soon enough, and I intend to be there waiting to summon them through before too many of the doomed jump to unnecessary deaths. So if you're thinking there's something to be done, I'd appreciate you getting to it. Unless, of course, you'd care to continue this meeting amidst a flood of refugees."

A barely perceptible shudder rippled through the group. None of them wanted to witness the General as she fed. Best to get this busines finished up quickly.

All eyes turned back to Vadoma, waiting.

"What's the plan?" the Grey Man asked.

Vadoma smiled and held up a purple gem that pulsed in her perfect hand with sickly internal light. The others recoiled from it in disgust, save McCaslin, who sat up a little straighter. "We recruit her to destroy this."

Holde Berge nodded. "And kill two birds with... two stones. I understand. But who among humanity is sick enough, evil enough, to wield that horror?"

"Do you not live in Nazi Germany, dearest?" Vadoma replied.

"You would put Merlin's Stone in the hands of those cretins?" The General's voice was deeper, her eyes grew dark.

"To save us from the power of the Guardians, I'd put Merlin themself in Goering's back pocket," Vadoma replied flatly.

"They'd probably get eaten," the General chuckled. The others weren't laughing. When the Righ made a joke about people getting eaten, no one else tended to find it very funny. "But in seriousness," she said, "that's a big risk. Too big. You should leave that here. Use a decoy."

Now it was Vadoma who was laughing.

"Oh, you would love to have your scaly fingers around Merlin's stone, wouldn't you?" she asked. It wasn't a question. If anything had the power to free the General from her faerie prison, an intact fetish spun by the person who'd locked the door to begin with could very well be that thing. Of course the Righ wanted it in her custody.

The General grinned in reply, her teeth appearing a little sharper than they had only a minute ago.

"You don't frighten me," Vadoma said. It might have been a lie. Nonetheless, the General stopped grinning. "And they would know if it's a fake. We have to use the real thing."

"Absolutely not!" Now it was the singer's turn to object. She stood from her seat and stamped her foot for emphasis. "It truly would be a thousand years of fascist rule, over human and Fäe alike, if they got that stone attuned."

"So they can't have it for long," the Grey Man piped up. "We don't give them the chance to perform the attenuation— or even to figure out how."

"No," Holde insisted. "It's still too much."

For the first time, Vadoma looked annoyed. "Even against the power of the labyrinth?"

Holde pursed her lips, but gave no answer.

"But how do we get her to chase it?" the Grey Man asked, twirling his carved salmon between his callused fingers.

"Like I said," Vadoma replied, "she's a true believer. We make her think she's saving the world."

"She really will be saving the world if you give that stone over to the Nazis," Holde reminded the others. "It won't just be some *schnitzeljagd*. You're putting all of us in real danger if you do this."

"Not all of us," McCaslin corrected.

The others glowered in her direction. She was correct, of course. What did one of her kind—a captive one at that—care if the mortal world went to shit? What even did she care if her faerie captors were conquered by the forces of global fascism?

"*Miststück*," Holde grumbled. She knew better than to challenge the Righ directly, but she was angry and she didn't care who knew it.

Vadoma quickly closed the space between them and took hold of the singer by her shoulders. It wouldn't do any of them any good to incite McCaslin's wrath.

"You are missing a piece of this puzzle, I think," she said.

"I am listening," Holde said back, her furious gaze still fixed on the General.

"They will never know what they have," Vadoma replied. "We tell the unwitting Guardian, of course," she continued, "we tell her about the power, and the dire stakes—we tell her she's saving humanity. But the Nazis...no."

"That makes sense," the General allowed. "Himmler's a zealot, but he's also a fool."

"If he is such a fool," Holde countered, "then why not a

decoy? Why do we dare put the true stone of Merlin into his hands?"

"My dear," replied Vadoma, moving her hands from the singer's shoulders to her face, "would you know on sight the difference between a genuine apple and one made of wood?"

"*Ja.*"

"And even," Vadoma continued, "were you to never have tasted an apple in your life, would you be able to discern which was fruit and which was inedible?"

Holde Berge met Vadoma's gaze for a moment, then could bear it no longer and looked down, chastened, giving an almost imperceptible nod.

"So you understand," Vadoma said. "He will know a thing of power when he sees it, but he will not know its nature, nor its origin, and when all is said and done, he and his acolytes will never know just how close they came to ruling the world." There was a tinkle of metal from her earrings as Vadoma looked back and forth between the others. "So we are in agreement, then?" she asked.

Holde and the Grey Man nodded. The General grinned through another puff of smoke.

"True believer she may be," the Grey Man said, "but still a mere mortal. We would have to hold her hand every step of the way. I prefer to keep out of the way of mortals, and to keep them out of mine."

Vadoma shrugged. "You will hold your nose and bear the

intrusion," she insisted. "Cover up the stench with the fish you love so much, if you must."

The Grey Man looked down at the carving in his hand, which had taken the shape of an Atlantic salmon.

Finally, he nodded, acquiescing as well. "We will have to expose our own pathways and escape routes—ways and means of passage we've kept secret for centuries. It's dangerous."

"It's not as dangerous as letting the Nazis have the stone," Berge insisted. "I would gladly show every mortal every secret we have if it meant keeping those beasts from that power."

"None of that matters," the General said, "does it?" The others turned to face her as she leaned forward in her seat, bracing her elbows on her knees as she addressed Vadoma. "Because she oughtn't live to tell the tale. That's your end-game, isn't it? You don't want an asset, you just want rid of a pest. You're not looking to recruit her, you're looking to dispose of her, and counting on the Nazis to do your dirty work."

"Clever as always," Vadoma said back.

"I appreciate your cunning, madam," McCaslin said, a peculiar smile crossing her face. "They wield the stone, break the protection of the Labyrinth, handle the Guardian before she knows what she is or what she's capable of. Then we come in to clean up whatever mess is left afterward."

"If she *is* left alive," Vadoma added, "it will be without the magic of the Labyrinth, and so we will have no trouble dispatching her in the aftermath."

The General stood, brushed her dress down, and blew a decidedly sarcastic smoke ring at them. "Get her to me," she instructed, suddenly taking charge of the room in a manner befitting the rank by which she'd been addressed for centuries. "Out of all of us I'm the easiest to find." She looked at Holde Berge, who suddenly seemed small beneath the General's gaze. "I'll get her to Berlin," the General said, "and I'll make sure she knows how to find my stone. I won't tell her to destroy it," McCaslin said then, her appearance once again wholly human, but somehow no less unsettling. She looked Vadoma in the eye and continued. "I get the stone, you get the Labyrinth, the Nazis take care of the girl."

"And if they don't," Vadoma added.

"We will," the General affirmed.

Around the room, each person nodded.

There was a rumble from beneath the floor. The Grey Man leapt to his feet.

"I'll get her to you, Your Highness," he said, bowing his head as he made for the door he'd come in through. Holde Berge was hot on his heels.

"I'll be awaiting her arrival," she stammered as she followed him through the door and onto the stairs leading out of the General's prison.

The two made their escape hurriedly, but Vadoma lingered. She approached The General and laid a hand on her arm. "I always thought that doing away with dragons was a mistake," she said.

The General smiled back at her. "I am still here, aren't I?"

Vadoma was frightened, but she stood fast.

"Feast well, Your Highness," she said in parting, "until we meet again."

Chapter 1

OCTOBER 1943
ARDARA, COUNTY DONEGAL
IRELAND

When the weather was nice, Pepper preferred to ride her bicycle into Ardara. It was a straight shot—or rather, as straight as shots could get on an Irish country road. The once-loose gravel had been well packed into the dirt by generations of cattle moving between pastures, and the hills rolled just gently enough to make the downhills fun while keeping the uphills from becoming too challenging. The way required little concentration and allowed Pepper's mind to wander all she cared to allow.

The Murphys, from whom she'd rented her small cottage, operated a dairy and she was welcome to hitch a ride aboard the milk lorry any time she pleased, but most of the time she preferred the open air and the time to think. Her enjoyment of the outdoors was one of the few things she'd been able to bring with her from back home in Seattle.

The nip of autumn was eking its way into the air more with each passing day. Soon, Pepper was sure, she'd be stowing the old Raleigh in the barn until spring. She knew she'd miss the ride when the time came.

Being in the out-of-doors felt a little bit like freedom—a commodity mostly lacking in Pepper's life of late. Her mind was welcome to wander on the old country road, but Pepper herself was quite planted for the time being.

Having to fake one's own death in order to give the slip to government operatives could do that to a trainee nurse.

Elsewhere, the world was at war. Just across the Celtic Sea the British were being subjected to aerial bombardment so horrifying that Pepper had a hard time even looking at the pictures in The Times. But here in Ireland, there was no such carnage. Thanks to the Irish government's official policy of neutrality, the island had been so far spared.

Pepper had occasionally stopped to wonder just how neutral her new home truly was; Allied aircraft were often seen overflying County Donegal. There seemed to be no such hospitality being extended to the Luftwaffe.

But that didn't matter so much to Pepper. It wasn't that she didn't care about the state of the world—it was just that there was nothing she could do about it, and bothering herself with international woes she had no way of influencing seemed an awful waste of time and energy.

When the sun was out, and the sea was calm, it was easy enough for Pepper Elizabeth Jones to forget all about the world's troubles.

Her own personal troubles weren't so easily dismissed.

Between the fact she was presumed dead, and the severity of the global conflict, she hoped the American authorities wouldn't bother looking for her. And even if they did—even if they learned of her presence in Ireland—the country's refusal to join the Allied cause meant the Americans would be unlikely to risk coming after her. If there was any silver lining to what was happening in Europe, Pepper figured that was it.

Plus, magic was free in Ireland—freer than perhaps anyplace else on the planet. Certainly magic was freer here than it was back home.

Which meant Pepper was free here, too. Free to understand fully what had happened to her—what was still happening to her.

She looked down at her wrist, where the old man's labyrinth dangled from an ordinary-looking bracelet. She had no idea the depth or the breadth of the magic this little item held. But she did know people had died for it. And she knew it had saved her life—that it would keep saving her life. It was the kind of power people would kill for.

So she would keep it safe. She would keep its *magic* safe.

After all, she was becoming increasingly convinced its unknown magics had been what led her to this place.

It had been an accident of train station timetables, transatlantic shipping, and the kindness of strangers that had brought Pepper to county Donegal, yet somehow she'd been positive she was in the right place from the moment she'd set foot in Ardara.

Plus: she liked Ardara. The weather was fair, and the people were friendly. She'd met the Murphys on her first day in town and had moved into their little cottage within the week. She enjoyed their company and appreciated that they hadn't cared to interrogate her. A young American woman relocating on her own to Ireland surely had a story to tell, they'd said once with a wink, but it wasn't a story they needed to know.

She'd come to view that generosity of discretion as both a blessing and a curse; she appreciated the privacy, but it would have been nice to have someone to tell her story to. And the old Irish couple would likely have even believed her.

She turned her bicycle onto the main street in Ardara town, careful to avoid running through any standing water from the previous night's rain. Ordinarily she wouldn't mind the puddles; there had been a time when she'd gleefully have ridden through them.

But lately she'd begun to mind keeping the hem of her

dress tidy. For no particular reason, of course. It surely wasn't for the boy who worked in the flower shop. Certainly not.

Her only errand for today was to the fishmonger. It wasn't that Pepper particularly cared for fish. In fact, she found the local seafood rather unimpressive compared to what she'd grown up with in coastal Washington state. But the fishmonger's shop had the distinct advantage of being located directly adjacent to the flower seller's.

Convenient, that.

Pepper turned off the main street and parked her bicycle in the usual spot in a narrow alley. She'd made a habit of parking in the alley because it kept her bicycle out of the flow of traffic and because it forced her to walk past the flower shop both coming and going. That meant double the chances to run into Sean Michael.

Pepper walked briskly back toward the main street, but cut her speed more than in half as she rounded the corner. She meandered past the florist shop, looking absently at the few blooms and green plants on stands outside the window. She hoped it wasn't too obvious—her hope to see the lad who worked there—so she didn't allow herself to tarry overlong. Far too soon, and without so much as a glimpse of Sean Michael, she was past the florist's shop and standing at the door to the fishmonger's.

Pepper took a deep breath before pulling open the door.

She'd braced herself, as always, to deal with the smell

of fish; it was always an unpleasant change after the sweet aromas of the flowers next door. Pepper's nose wrinkled out of sheer habit, but she realized almost instantly that today there was no odor at all.

And it wasn't just that the smell of fish was missing.

The aromas of salt and of disinfectant, of metal polish, sealing wax, and vinegar—all of them were entirely absent. There was no smell at all in this place.

Pepper found that odd.

The oddness compounded itself when Pepper spotted a stranger behind the counter. The Byrnes had occasionally hired local fellows to help in the shop, but they'd always been lads Pepper had recognized from town. But this man wasn't from town. She'd been in Ardara long enough to know its faces, and this one was new.

The stranger was tall and gangly, with biceps that bulged beneath his dingy gray linen shirt. A linen shirt seemed a peculiar choice for working behind a fish counter, but that was hardly the most curious thing about his presence.

"Good morning to you," the stranger greeted in an accent Pepper couldn't quite place. "I've your order all prepped and ready." The stranger turned his back then, and set to work on something Pepper couldn't see.

"Hi," Pepper said back, "good morning. It's nice to meet you. But I'm afraid you have me mistaken for someone else."

"No," the man replied, not so much bothering to turn

around and face her, "no mistake."

"But I didn't order..." Pepper's protestation was stopped short when the man turned around, bringing with him a large parcel wrapped in brown paper and tied with string. It was long and narrow, and reminded Pepper of the parcels of whole salmon her mother had sometimes brought home when she was a child. Seeing as she was in a fish market, Pepper figured that could be precisely what the paper parcel contained.

She frowned squarely at it.

"Here you are," the fellow said, placing the parcel on the counter in front of him.

Pepper shook her head and took a step back.

"That's not my order."

"It is. It's yours. Take it."

"No," Pepper argued. "That is an enormous fish. And I don't know how many times I need to tell you that I didn't order it. It would take me all week to eat a fish that size and even if I was interested in eating the same fish every day for a week, I'm really not interested in paying for a giant fish I didn't order. Also," she went on, crossing her arms over her chest, "I have never met you before and I honestly don't know why you think you know who I am, much less why you think you know that I ordered this fish, which, I repeat, I did not."

"There's no charge," the man assured her, pushing the wrapped fish across the counter toward her. "It's your fish.

You should take it."

Pepper shook her head again.

"Where are the Byrnes?" She quizzed. "Are they all right? Did you do something to them? Do they know you're in here insisting on giving away their fish for free?"

The man leaned forward, bracing himself against the counter with his forearm and looking Pepper squarely in the eye.

"The Byrnes are all right," he said, "and this is for you. Paid in full. You should take it."

There was a gleam in his eye. Or a glint. Or a flash; something unnatural made Pepper feel all at once terribly unsettled and completely reassured. The labyrinth suddenly felt warm against her wrist. Whatever was going on here, she didn't like it, and the only way she could think of to make it stop was to take the damned fish. Maybe she'd toss it in the gutter just as soon as she was out of the shop, but she needed to get out of the shop first. And she had a sneaking suspicion she wasn't going to be allowed to leave without the creepy stranger's paper-wrapped gift.

She stepped forward and snatched the parcel from the counter, retreating to a somewhat safer distance as quickly as her feet would take her.

"Thank you," she said, not really meaning it.

Pepper looked down at the fish. Something about the heft of the thing and the feel of the paper in her hands felt right and proper. It was a feeling not unlike she'd had when she'd first put on the labyrinth.

Damn.

As secure as that feeling was at its core, it unsettled Pepper at a gut level. She knew this feeling—this feeling of abiding magic and connection. She knew it intimately. But in the few short months since she'd taken possession of the labyrinth, she had yet to grow comfortable with it.

Her unease was amplified when she looked back up to find no sign of the gentleman who had only a moment before been behind the counter.

Pepper couldn't get out of there fast enough. She turned on her heel and was out the door before she could think too much about where the stranger might have gone.

Chapter 2

Pepper dashed uncharacteristically quickly down the sidewalk and past the flower shop. She'd normally have dithered a bit in hopes of seeing her crush, but there was something about the presence of this damnable fish that made her want to get the hell out of town.

She'd nearly made it to the corner when she heard a familiar voice call out to her from behind.

"G'mornin' to ye, Miss Jones!"

Pepper squeezed her eyes shut. She'd need to think fast. She considered for a moment pretending she hadn't heard him, scurrying off around the corner with her puzzled face and overlarge fish and apologizing for it the next time she came to town.

But she was sure she'd started enough at the sound of his voice for him to know she'd heard. And if he knew she'd heard, then he'd know she was lying about not having heard. And Pepper figured he was liable to take that personally. And that just wouldn't do.

She liked him, and she didn't want to hurt his feelings.

Besides: holding a gigantic fish was hardly a reason not to talk to a person in Ardara.

Pepper stopped and turned to face him, hoping any disquiet would read as nothing more than trouble handling a fish of such size all on her own.

"Hi," she said, trying her best to sound like nothing out of the ordinary was happening.

"How are things?" he asked.

For a moment, Pepper was tempted to tell him the truth. She was currently in possession of a fish she'd neither wanted nor paid for, given to her by a probably-magical stranger, she wasn't entirely certain just how she was supposed to get the damned thing home in the little basket of her bicycle, and she had no small degree of worry for the health and well-being of the Byrne family.

But that was probably not the level of question he'd really been asking.

"Good," she lied, plastering enough of a smile onto her face she figured he'd likely be fooled until her real smile showed up. And her real smile always showed up when she saw Sean Michael. She really couldn't help it.

A gust off the water blew a lock of hair into Pepper's face.

She absently brushed it away with her right hand, nearly losing her grip on the fish when she did. As she struggled to get purchase on it again, Sean Michael stepped forward, taking hold of the fish from below and helping to steady it in Pepper's hands.

Sean Michael was a strapping lad, only a few years younger than Pepper as best she could tell, but with a fresh-off-the-farm naivete that she couldn't help but be charmed by. It was a harmless flirtation, and Pepper was sure nothing would ever come of it. Still, seeing him on her trips to town brought some joy into her day. Joy was in short supply in the world these days, and Pepper was determined to cling to it wherever it presented itself.

Joy with a sweet smile and dimples was especially welcome.

And as best she could tell, Sean Michael seemed to like smiling at her as much as she enjoyed smiling at him. If he'd ever noticed her manner as giddy or awkward, he hadn't mentioned as much. She liked him; he was sweet, and he was handsome, and she liked him.

And he was, in this moment, standing far closer to her than he ever had before.

"Thanks," she managed to say, sounding slightly out of breath as she felt a flush rising to her cheeks. She gripped the fish a little tighter as she took a small step backward, hoping a little distance might allay any further blushing on her part.

Pepper Jones had handled a breakout from a government detention camp, the illicit crossing of multiple international borders, and the guardianship of what she guessed to be the most powerful magical item she'd ever so much as heard of; she was sure the day would come when she could handle herself in the presence of an attractive flower seller.

But today was apparently not that day.

"You've got your hands full there," Sean Michael said.

"It's a fish," Pepper replied—quite possibly the most awkward phrase she'd uttered in her adult life.

"Aye, that it is," he agreed, "A big fish. Might you be entertaining?"

Pepper's eyes grew wide and her mouth dropped open. It hadn't occurred to her until that very moment she was carrying far too much fish for a single person to eat on their own before it spoiled. The last thing she wanted was for him to think she'd be cooking for a gentleman caller.

"Oh, no," she replied. "I just... I couldn't leave it in the shop." It wasn't a lie. So what if Sean Michael didn't completely understand? "I'll probably wind up sharing it with the Murphys." She managed a smile then, hoping she'd satisfied Sean Michael's curiosity in a way that didn't upset the proverbial apple cart between them.

"Ah," Sean Michael replied, smiling then in that way that made his dimple show and Pepper's heart do a little fluttery thing in her chest. "May I help you with that?" he offered.

Pepper forced an even bigger smile.

On the one hand she'd be happy to have a second set of hands to help her secure the overlarge parcel to her bicycle. But on the other hand, she'd soundly discovered that her befuddlement at having been gifted the thing had made her even more awkward than usual. The more time she spent in his company, the more chance she had to make an idiot out of herself in the eyes of Sean Michael.

But in the end her clumsiness won out over her awkwardness.

Whatever was up with the stranger in the shop, it was almost certainly magical in nature, and she was becoming convinced she needed to take the thing home and at least unwrap it.

The labyrinth had gotten consistently warmer against her wrist since she'd taken possession of the parcel—likely a portent of its significance.

But how in the name of the wind was she going to get the massive fish home on her bicycle?

Pepper foisted the heavy thing into Sean Michael's outstretched arms and led him around to the alley where her bicycle was parked. Maybe he'd have some idea.

"I guess I wasn't really thinking about getting it home," she said, looking back and forth between the fish and her bike.

"You'll be fine," Sean Michael assured her. He jostled the

fish in his arms, as though trying to figure its weight. He smiled at Pepper again, then stepped forward and deposited the bulky thing in the bicycle's basket.

Pepper couldn't believe her eyes—the damned thing fit!

The fish's spine managed to curve sideways just enough to rest on its side on the basket's bottom, with the head and tail both sticking out a good deal on both ends, but not far enough that Pepper thought it would be any impediment to steering on her way home.

"Thank you," she said, still marveling at how perfectly the fish had fit into the space.

"You're welcome."

The two of them stood there, rather awkwardly, for a moment before Pepper moved to get onto her bike.

"I'd better get this home," she said.

"Just a minute," Sean Michael said, reaching out and taking her arm before she had a chance to climb aboard the cycle. He held up a single finger in her direction and added, "I'll be right back, please wait here?" before turning and dashing off back in the direction of the main street.

"Okay?" Pepper replied.

She hardly had a moment to wonder what Sean Michael was up to before he was back in front of her.

"I've somethin' for ye," he said.

This time, Pepper's smile was genuine.

In his hand, Sean Michael held the most perfect miniature

tea rose she had ever seen. It was an incredibly vibrant, yet pale shade of pink, with tightly-wound petals blossoming in a gorgeous spiral and two tiny leaves flanking its narrow stem.

"It's beautiful," she said.

"A lovely for the lovely," Sean Michael said as he approached Pepper and slid the flower into the buttonhole in the lapel of her jacket. That was far bolder a statement of fondness than he'd made in her direction up to now. Now it was Sean Michael's turn for his cheeks to flush. Pepper liked that. She stood still and let him fasten the flower with a pin he'd pulled from his apron.

"I shall wear it with pride," she said, bending her head to give the flower a sniff. It smelled as wonderfully as it looked, and Pepper couldn't hide her delight. Buttonholes as nice as this one could go for quite a sum, but Sean Michael had chosen instead to give it to her. "And every time I look down, I'll think again of the dear boy who's given me such a thoughtful gift."

Sean Michael's cheeks flushed further; he was nearly the color of the little rose as he took a step backward and wrung his hands in his apron.

"I'm glad you like it," he said quietly.

"I adore it," she replied, "thank you. And thank you for your help with the fish." Pepper crossed in his direction until she was close enough to lean in and kiss his cheek.

He seemed to melt a little at that, and Pepper decided now would be an excellent time to hit the road. She had a paper-wrapped mystery to get to the bottom of; standing here flirting wasn't going to do her any good in that regard. "I'll see you soon," she said, turning then and crossing back to where her bicycle was parked.

When she looked back at Sean Michael, he was still smiling.

"Soon, then," he agreed. "In fact, keep wearing that flower and it might be sooner than you think." Then he winked.

Pepper was glad to have her bicycle beneath her as her knees went slightly weak at the gesture. She smiled back and nodded as she turned towards home and began to pedal.

As she rode past, she thought she saw Sean Michael pass the flower shop and head for the door of the fishmonger's. She wondered if he was going to ask about her, and what the gray man would tell him. Maybe she'd ask when she saw him next. Pepper looked down at the fish in the basket of her bike and shook her head.

Probably not.

Chapter 3

Horton McDavish's desk had never been clean. From the day he'd been given this office—this cavernous chamber in the attic of Bletchley Park Manor—every available surface had been occupied with some pile of paperwork or another. It confounded him, sometimes, how chaos always seemed to reign on the top of his desk, when in all other ways he thought himself such an orderly fellow. Stout and stocky, with ginger hair and a handlebar moustache, he was normally so tidy as to be a proper caricature of a British Government man.

He figured magic to be the root of the mayhem. Magic, as far as he could tell, was the opposite of order. And since the start of the war the Arcane Intelligence Division had been at its most tumultuous. Just this week the Kiwis had sent a poorly-coded telegram regarding the possible use of a powerful magical item within their borders.

The very thought of being asked to investigate further turned Horton's stomach a little. The number of miles to be traveled over land, air, and sea (ugh...sea) would be daunting even in peacetime. But having to traverse multiple theatres of combat made it unappealing to the extreme.

And it wasn't as though this revelation was entirely new to him.

The British had word of this item's discovery as early as 1928, possibly going back to '27, but the Baldwin government just hadn't cared much about magic. McDavish had been instructed to "keep an eye on the situation," whatever that meant. It was under Chamberlain that Britain had really begun to investigate magic as a tool that could be used in furtherance of the British Empire, but it wasn't until Churchill had taken office that the Arcane Intelligence Department had evolved into its current state. Using magic in service of the British war effort had been a key plank in the Prime Minister's platform from the beginning.

It was an idea he'd borrowed from the Americans, and the reason Horton McDavish had been elevated from his position as a one-man department relegated to an unassuming desk in London to this well-supplied office in the heart of the British Intelligence Apparatus.

Since then, he'd had much more pressing, and much more local issues to deal with than goings on in New Zealand.

"Horton!" his partner called to him, pushing open his office door without bothering to knock. "A call's just come in. It's being decoded now. I think this could be it!"

McDavish looked up at the intruder and gave a nod.

If magic was the opposite of order, Cavill Weathersby was the opposite of Horton McDavish. Tall and lanky, clean-shaven, with unruly black hair and his suit always in need of a proper pressing, Cav was as American as Horton could imagine a person being. He'd been sent to Bletchley from Washington D.C. on the trail of an item not unlike the one known to be in New Zealand.

The item had crossed borders and changed hands wildly and in rapid succession not long after the attack on Pearl Harbor had brought America's support of the British war effort out of hiding. And America was paying close enough attention to know about it while it was happening. They'd managed to ascertain the item had come into the possession of a young woman, and they had a pretty accurate description of her at that.

But what they hadn't been able to do was tail her effectively.

The FBI had lost her trail pretty soon after they'd picked it up, and it had been Cavill Weathersby and his colleagues in the OSS Arcane Division who had been tasked with finding it again. Several of the men on the Arcane Desk in Washington were still quite occupied with searching for the item and its custodian within the United States, but Cav (possibly through some magic talents of his own—Horton was far too polite to ask) had determined the woman and her totem had crossed the proverbial pond and he had been subsequently assigned to McDavish's division at Bletchley Park to continue the search.

That talisman could be of vital service to the Allied war effort.

Having determined—thanks to the ongoing and assiduous British intelligence gathering apparatus—that the item was absolutely not on the Island of Great Britain, Weathersby had turned his attention across the channel to Ireland. A neutral country with no obligation to cooperate with either American or British authorities, and a place where magic was known to be free and unregulated, the Emerald Isle seemed a logical place for a person who wished to lay low.

"You think really?" Horton asked, standing from his desk. Whether or not they were making progress on their American quarry, anything to take his mind off New Zealand was welcome.

"I think really, yeah," Cav replied. "All I know's I got told there's something about flowers."

"Hrmph," Horton sounded, crossing his arms over his chest as he followed Cav out the door and onto the narrow staircase. Maybe.

Flower was the code name of the fellow the American

OSS had sent to Ireland. He was Irish by lineage, American by birth, and a magic user of some variety. That was all Horton McDavish knew of the man; rather, that and the fact they'd not heard a word from him in the months since his deployment.

Horton presumed Cav must know more than he did. He'd spent enough time in the Intelligence Service to know better than to ask questions. Things in this office were need-to-know, and Horton presumed he just didn't need to know... yet.

He followed his partner through the main floor hallway and into an operations room, past one of the ubiquitous blue *Do Not Help The Enemy* signs.

"Is it here yet?" Cav called out to no one in particular.

"They're just running it over from the Cipher Office now," a dark-haired woman answered, hanging up a telephone and turning her attention back to her typewriter. The nameplate on her desk identified her as Beatrice Camberwinkle, lead clerk.

"It's coming from the Cipher Office," Cav said, turning to Horton and waggling his eyebrows. This was Cavill Weathersby's first message traffic through the Cipher Office and he was far too American to hide his enthusiasm for it.

He had tailed this dame and the trinket she carried across a continent and then across an ocean. And he had a very strong feeling he was about to know for sure where she'd been hiding since he lost her scent several months ago. He fidgeted in spite of himself as he turned his attention toward the doorway.

"Keep hold of yourself, lad," Horton admonished him quietly. "We're all professionals here."

Cav frowned at his partner and continued to fidget. He danced beneath himself, shoving his hands in and out of his pockets, until a young woman carrying a manila envelope came through the door. He reached out to take the envelope, but the girl brushed by as though she hadn't so much as seen him there.

She approached the desk by the window and handed her parcel over to the office's Lead Clerk.

"Thank you, Louise," she said.

"You're welcome," Louise answered, smiling at the other woman before turning to leave.

Cav wrung his hands at his waist and looked expectantly at the envelope. Beatrice paid him no mind. She pulled a ledger from out of her desk drawer, opened the envelope, and recorded the delivery.

"Here you are, Mr. Weathersby," she said, slipping the page back into the envelope and holding it out across her desk.

Cav was there in two strides. He snatched the envelope and yanked the page out from inside.

"Thank you, Beatrice," Horton said, frowning in the

direction of his impolite partner. But Cav didn't hear him.

"Ardara!" Cav yelled. He flipped the page around so Horton could see, but his hand was shaking so intensely the typed words were completely illegible. "Our girl is in Ardara!" he shouted, louder this time.

Horton grabbed Cavill by his arm and spun him around, pointing at the bright blue sign on the wall.

```
DON'T HELP THE ENEMY
CARELESS TALK
MAY GIVE AWAY
VITAL SECRETS
```

"Keep it down, man," McDavish insisted.

"She's in Ardara," Cav said back, quietly, "County Donegal in Ireland." Horton's hand still on his arm, Cav led them out of the bustling operations room and into an empty hallway. "We know where she is," he said, shoving the page toward his partner. Horton took hold of the page to read it for himself.

It was blank.

"What the hell are you on about?" Horton asked, turning the page around.

Cav shook his head. He took the page and shoved it back in the envelope.

"She's in Ardara," he said again, "it says so right there."

"It said nothing of the sort," Horton argued. "In fact," he added, "it said nothing at all. I have no idea what it is you're referring to."

"Never mind that," Cav insisted. He reached into the

pocket of his rumpled corduroy blazer and brought out a hinged metal box. It reminded Horton very much of a folded daguerreotype his mother had kept of her grandparents.

Cav opened the hinge slowly, revealing a green velvet lining on one side, and a glass-covered compartment on the other. Beneath the glass there were scattered pieces of what looked like dried flowers—a jumble of leaves and petals with no sort of order or reason to how they were arranged.

"Wassat?" Horton asked, bending his head to get a better look at the thing. He still had no idea what it was.

"It's a Compass Rose," Cav answered, his eyes fixed on the dried plants beneath the glass.

"Of course," Horton grumbled, "it's a compass rose." He shook his head and frowned at Cavill. "What the hell is a compass rose?"

"Just watch," Cav said, his voice almost a whisper as he balanced the strange item on his palm.

Horton blew out his cheeks with a huff. What exactly was he supposed to be watching? This bunch of dead flowers inside a picture frame held his interest not at all. He was convinced it was going to be another case of Cav seeing a message on a blank sheet of typing paper.

But then he saw it.

One pink petal at first, and then the next, the little tea rose seemed to be coming back to life. The petals brightened and they plumped, they curled and ruffled at the edges, and they began to coalesce into their proper shape. The leaves followed, growing thicker and greener—even their veins pullulating with chlorophyll.

Horton McDavish was mesmerized.

And he was terrified.

In his job in the Arcane Intelligence Service, Horton had seen pages and pages of reports on magic: on its uses and users, on its possibilities and limitations. He'd read countless accounts of magical people, places, things, and occurrences. But he'd never actually seen magic with his own two eyes.

He figured it must be much the same as a man having read extensively on the sea finally seeing the shore for himself.

"Good God," he said.

"Uh-huh," Cavill affirmed, nodding his head as he began to smile. "This is a Compass Rose," he repeated himself. "Flower's got our girl pinned in Ardara," he said, "and we're going to go get her."

Chapter 4

The ride home from town was usually taken at a leisurely pace. Having handled whatever business had brought her into Ardara to begin with, Pepper liked to ride back slowly, occasionally turning off the main road to explore. County Donegal was a treasure trove of ancient and beautiful things—both natural and man-made.

There were fascinating old buildings, giant shade trees, and beautiful fields of heather just off the main road, and Pepper was keen on exploring all of them. There was magic in this land, she was sure, and it just felt right, and good, to take the time to try and seek it out.

But not today. Today, it seemed, the magic had sought her out instead.

That magic, in the form of an overlarge fish, had her pedaling home much faster than usual. Her curiosity was piqued and her hackles were up.

Every so often, the wind would catch the flower in her lapel just so, delivering the heavenly smell of tea rose to her nostrils—a far more pleasant scent than that of the fish just upwind in her bicycle basket.

She pulled onto the long driveway of the Murphy farm and held her breath as she sped past the main house and barn. If Mr. Murphy was out, there was a good a chance as not that he'd flag her down. And that just wouldn't do this afternoon.

Pepper liked the man, and she was grateful to him and his wife for having taken her in so readily when she'd been in such dire need of a place to lay her head. She'd spent many an afternoon since coming to Ardara helping out with some minor farm chore or another just so Mr. Murphy would have someone to listen to his stories. Most days she didn't mind, but today she had a mysterious fish in her bicycle basket and a burning desire to see what the hell was up with it.

Pepper let herself exhale when she saw the milk truck was missing from its usual spot beside the barn. The Murphys were gone for the afternoon

She rode quickly past the main house and right up to the doorway of her cottage. She'd take the bike back into the barn later. There was no rain on the horizon; the old Raleigh would be safe in the open for the time being.

Getting inside with the fish proved less of a chore than

she'd feared. What to do next took a little more figuring out. Pepper frowned as she considered her options.

The cottage kitchen was small: a sink and a stove, a handful of cabinets, and barely enough counter space to dry the day's dishes on.

Her first inclination was to roll up the rug and see to the fish on the floor. But she worried that the old varnish wasn't up to the task of keeping any stray fish drippings from seeping into the planks; the very last thing she wanted out of this whole ordeal was a lifetime of fish smell in her cottage.

The kitchen table was a better choice, as it was made of very modern Formica. The problem with the table was its size. Barely three feet square; it seemed inadequate to the task. One end or the other was going to hang off the edge.

But still, it was the best option she had.

Pepper dropped the overlarge parcel onto the yellow surface and nodded. She took off her jacket carefully, taking a moment to smell the pretty flower in her lapel before draping it over the back of one of the matching dinette chairs. She un-clasped the bracelet containing the Labyrinth from her wrist and slid it into her jacket pocket; it wouldn't do for such a powerful arcane item to end up covered in fish guts.

Rolling up her sleeves as she went, Pepper fetched a large knife from her kitchen drawer.

The knife was dull, but it would do.

Once she was through the twine around it, Pepper pulled

slowly at the paper—careful not to tear it, as she had little else about the cottage to wrap the portions in when this was all done.

The fish itself was a salmon, she discovered. It looked remarkably similar to the Columbia River salmon she'd grown up enjoying. Odd, she thought, that a fish in Washington and a fish in Ireland can look so similar to one another. But she was grateful to at least have recognized the thing for what it was—and that it was something she knew how to clean and how to cook.

Pepper was pleased to find it had seen a knife already. It had been scaled and gutted, leaving Pepper with only the task of portioning it into fillets. It surprised her how much that fact elevated her mood. She hadn't realized just how much she was dreading having to deal with the scales and the guts of a fish this size all on her own. Growing up, it had always been her father's task to deal with the icky parts of the salmon.

Still, she was going to have to remove the fish's head. There were plenty of people in the world who didn't mind the head so much—some who would even leave it attached to the fish while it cooked. Pepper Elizabeth Jones was not one of those people.

The fish head would go out back to the Murphys' hogs in short order.

"Here goes," she said quietly to herself as she lowered

her dull kitchen knife to a spot just behind the gills. It was a guess; Pepper hadn't ever cut the head off a fish before, but she'd seen the result plenty of times. And she didn't so much care if she lost a little meat in the process; there was far more fish here than she figured she'd be able to eat. A little waste wasn't really a concern.

As Pepper made the first cut into the salmon's silver-flecked skin, a tiny roll of pristine white paper came peeking out of the fish's mouth.

It was odd enough to see what was clearly a human-fashioned item coming out of the mouth of a dead fish on her kitchen table, but the fact it was a pure, bright white and lacked even the slightest hint of having been mussed by its time in the animal's gullet was outright bizarre.

"Well, damn," she whispered, bending her head to get a closer look.

This had to be the reason for the fish. This had to be what the man in the shop had meant to give her.

"Solve a mystery with another mystery... I guess."

Pepper set down the knife and reached for the paper, pulling it gingerly from its fishy carrel. The whole thing was maybe four inches in length, rolled tightly and tied with a green and purple ribbon, and showed no signs of ever having been in water—much less inside a salmon.

A chill ran up Pepper's spine as she examined the scroll.

Careful not to get fish on her jacket, she reached into

its pocket and withdrew her bracelet. The Labyrinth felt as warm as a fresh pot of tea as she held it in her hand. She was shaking as she held the Labyrinth and the scroll side-by-side.

When looked at on end, the rolled paper's lines precisely matched the lines of the Labyrinth. Had she dipped the two in ink, the stamps they'd have made would have been indistinguishable from one another.

For the first time this whole thing was beginning to make sense. Whatever this scroll was, whatever the strange man in the shop had meant by its giving, it was connected to the Labyrinth.

And the Labyrinth was connected to her.

Suddenly this felt bigger than the fish.

Still holding the toasty-warm Labyrinth in her hand, Pepper slipped the ribbon from the scroll and pulled it open.

The paper smelled of cedar and pine, not at all of fish guts or saltwater. Somehow Pepper was not surprised.

She started to read the thing out loud, but stopped herself. If this paper contained an incantation, she'd do well to know what was there before speaking it. She knew already there was magic involved; the very last thing she needed was to accidentally conjure an ancient evil or summon some sort of fairytale monster into her cottage kitchen.

She read it to herself silently.

General McCaslin

20A Temple Bar

Dublin 2

The name and address were written in script—the kind Pepper always associated with the Declaration of Independence. And then, beneath them, a hastily scrawled note in pencil simply read:

Come quickly!

Pepper wasn't sure what she'd expected to see when she opened the scroll, but as she read the words, she was sure this wasn't it. She set the scroll down on the table in front of her and shook her head.

Was she really supposed to drop everything, including this massive fish, and go to Dublin?

She decided that was completely preposterous. There was absolutely no way she was about to embark on such an intensive errand at the behest of an unsolicited note from the mouth of a fish.

The scroll suddenly grew white-hot in her hand. She opened her fingers instinctively, dropping it onto the table in front of her. By the time it landed, it had curled back in on itself and had once again taken a shape identical to the lines of the Labyrinth.

"God damn it," Pepper grumbled, sinking into the chair where her jacket was hung. She didn't like it one bit, but she was going to Dublin. To number 20-A Temple Bar. To see someone named General McCaslin.

Pepper turned her head to look at the clock on her wall. It was late afternoon already; the last bus out of Ardara had left for the day. But if she got to bed early, she'd be able to get into town in time for the first bus in the morning.

That was going to have to be the plan.

But first she was going to eat her fill of salmon.

Chapter 5

The morning chill was still lingering over the country-side as Pepper locked the door to her cottage and started for town. The day was shaping up to be a dreary one—the kind she'd come to expect from Ireland in autumn. It made her just a little homesick. The dampness and abiding gloom reminded her so much of the colder months back home she could sometimes even forget just how far away she truly was.

But not on this morning.

On this morning she was just about as far from the safety and familiarity of home and family as she could imagine. She surely had never foreseen herself in the role of an international fugitive. And she was reasonably certain no one had ever aspired to be sent on an errand by a salmon.

But here she was—both of those things. Pepper tried her best not to think too hard about that and instead did her best to focus on the immediate task; she needed to get to Ardara in time for the first bus to Donegal and she needed to do it on foot.

She hadn't slept well; questions about strange fish and magical labyrinths kept her up for most of the night—and the Murphy's rooster had seen to it she woke with the dawn. It was all her addled brain could do to remember to put her cash and a small parcel of crackers into her bag for the trip.

She probably could have done with more and better supplies considering the length of the trip ahead, but assembling those would take time. The note had said to come quickly, so that was what she was going to do. She would just have to make do with what she had on hand.

She set off for town in her best approximation of a traveling suit: an ivory blouse, tan skirt, her most comfortable shoes, her favorite hat, and lace gloves. She was happy as she walked that she'd tossed on her brown tweed jacket, with her flower from Sean Michael still fastened in the lapel. The flower had fared remarkably well in the chilly autumn night, and it still looked as bright and as lovely as it had when he'd first presented it to her. Looking down at the perfect pink blossom lifted Pepper's mood a bit as she made her way to town through the October gray.

The bus to Donegal was already loading when Pepper reached the corner of the main street where it stopped. It occurred to her as she approached the driver where he stood on the sidewalk that she hadn't the foggiest idea what a ticket was going to cost her.

She could only hope the wad of cash she'd grabbed this morning would be enough for the round trip, or that the salmon had return bus fare waiting for her at number 20-A Temple Bar.

"One to Dublin?" she asked when she reached the front of the short queue.

The driver shook his head.

"Only as far as Donegal, miss," he said, "You'll buy your fare to Dublin at the station when you arrive."

"All right." Pepper nodded. She reached into her purse and handed over a coin for the fare to Donegal. The Labyrinth grew warm against her wrist as she waited for the driver to hand back her ticket and allow her to board.

Ticket in hand, Pepper stepped to the side to get out of the way of other patrons while she put away her remaining cash. As she struggled to shut her overstuffed purse, she happened to look up, only to catch Sean Michael looking at her from outside the flower shop on the far corner of main street.

He waved when he noticed her looking.

Pepper felt her face flush. How long had he been looking at her? She juggled her still-open purse, trying to free one hand or the other to wave back. By the time she got her hand in the air, he had already turned to go back inside.

Pepper frowned to herself. She hoped she hadn't hurt his

feelings. But she didn't have time to dwell on that. She wrangled her purse closed and turned back to the task at hand. She climbed aboard the mostly-empty bus and found a seat near the back.

It was only a few minutes more before the driver took his seat, shut the door, and cranked the engine.

Pepper hadn't thought to ask ahead of time how long the ride to Donegal from Ardara was likely to take. She wasn't even sure if the bus made stops between the two towns. But it wasn't like she had any say in the matter, and she decided not to be bothered with the details.

The note had said to come quickly, and this bus was the quickest way to go. It would have to be enough.

The Donegal town bus was a lumbering thing, with a poor suspension, drafty windows, and singularly uncomfortable seats. Stopping every few miles to pick up and let off passengers, it was by no measure an efficient means of transport. Horton McDavish hadn't been sure what he'd been expecting when he and Cavill had been told that would be their way into the town center from the airfield on the city's outskirts, but this had definitely not been it.

He'd always been prone to impatience and had spent much of his life learning to squelch the outward indications of such. His natural aversion to inefficiencies had rarely shown itself as profoundly as it did on that morning's ride. It seemed every time the bus got into gear and up to speed, it nigh immediately began to slow again. Adding to his impatience was the impatience of his partner, which was manifesting itself in an abject inability to stay still in his seat.

He'd been antsy since before their plane had taken off in the predawn hours of the morning. Cavill Weathersby was a man as excitable as he was inexperienced, and his elated satisfaction at learning of the RAF's secret array of airfields had been more than Horton could abide so early in the day.

Horton, who had never been at all comfortable with flying, had done his best to mask his annoyance at his partner's unambiguous enthusiasm right along with his own nerves. The only thing he found at all reassuring about this trip was the proximity of their destination to his desk at Bletchley Park. Chasing a trinket across the sea and over the road into the Irish countryside beat chasing one all the way to New Zealand any day.

The Service only needed access to one of these charms. And if there was one to be had this close to home, what was a little discomfort in the service of King and Country?

Still, he was finding the bus ride interminable.

Horton looked beside himself at his fidgeting partner. Cav was holding the Compass Rose between his palms and wore a grin on his face that Horton found quite incomprehensible.

"You're far too chipper for given circumstances," Horton

said softly. Cav shook his head.

"And you're not chipper enough," he said back. "We balance each other out."

"You are mercurial and undisciplined," Horton said.

"And you're a fuddy-duddy."

"I am a professional," Horton countered, "and an Englishman. I have neither burning curiosity nor any intense enthusiasm for today's undertaking. This isn't my hobby," he continued, "it's my profession. I have a duty to perform, and I shall perform said duty to the best of my ability. But I am in no way required to grow excited by the work."

"Yeah, all right," Cav allowed. "Could you at lest express a little pleasure at the fact that we're only spending half an hour on a bus today instead of seven or eight?"

Horton nodded.

The plan had been to take the RAF Lancastrian across the Irish Sea, landing in Donegal, where they'd take the town bus to the main depot and catch an intercity bus on to Ardara. But they'd been intercepted at the Donegal airfield by a clerk with a telephone message.

```
NO NEED FOR LAST LEG
SPICE AND TRINKET ON MORNNG BUS
INTERCEPT AT DONEGAL STATION
FLOWER
```

It had been a cryptic enough message that the fellow manning the telephone surely hadn't understood its meaning. Working a secret RAF airfield in the midst of an ever-growing global conflict, he probably hadn't thought anything of it. But the missive's intended recipients were clear enough on what it meant.

As the town bus rounded the final corner and pulled into the main depot, Horton could admit to himself that he was, indeed, thankful for the abbreviated travel plan. He'd spent quite enough travel time already.

The moment the conveyance had come to a stop, Cav was up and into the aisle. It only took him four strides to cover the length of the bus. He scrambled down the stairs, onto the sidewalk, and into the depot. By the time Horton had caught up to him, he was skulking just around a corner from the ticket window.

He had the Compass Rose open flat on his palm and his gaze was darting back and forth between its face and the queue at the ticket counter.

"Anything?" Horton asked.

"Shhhh!" Cav admonished, putting out his hand to block his partner's path. Then he pointed, subtly but definitely, at a dark-haired young woman standing at the ticketing window. Her back was to them, but Cav had seen enough to be sure. "That's her."

"Just there?" Horton asked, his gaze following the woman as she slipped something into her handbag and stepped away from the ticket counter.

"Yeah," Cav replied, looking down at the Compass Rose

and back up again, "that's her. That's Ms. Jones." He closed the hinge on the device and put it back in his pocket. "We've got to be careful about this," he said quietly, tilting his head toward Horton, but never taking his eyes off Pepper.

"You think she'll know who you are?"

"I don't think so," Cav answered, moving slowly around the corner to keep an eye on Miss Jones as she walked farther away. "I don't think she ever saw my face before. But she's slippery. And she's got good instincts."

"You think she'll run again?"

"I do. And I haven't come this far just to lose track of her again."

"We'll need to get her alone," Horton reminded his partner as they stepped further into the lobby of the depot. "We cannot just approach her in the midst of a crowded depot...."

"Do you think I don't know this stuff's classified?" Cav asked, shaking his head. "We just need to corner her without her ever feeling cornered." He continued his slow but deliberate pursuit, keeping constant distance between himself and Jones, and trying his best to look as though he didn't notice when she turned her head around.

If she realized two men were on her tail, this day was going to get a lot harder.

Chapter 6

*A*lthough she was feeling oddly fine, Pepper was sure she looked a mess as her bus came to a stop at the Donegal depot. She could see her skirt was rumpled and she could feel the tweed imprint in her right cheek. There was also every chance she'd managed to smash her hat a bit, seeing as she hadn't been bothered to take it off. She was pleased to note, however, that the flower in her lapel had survived the bus ride unscathed, even though she'd spent the majority of the trip leaning haphazardly against the windowsill, watching the Irish countryside out the window as they went by. She took a refreshing sniff of its still-delightful fragrance as she moved to disembark.

The ticket counter was at the far end of the station from the bay where the Ardara bus had pulled in, with a large timetable above it and an equally large clock beside.

The next bus to Dublin left in a little over an hour; provided it wasn't sold out, Pepper would make it to her destination sometime in the late evening. She approached the ticket counter and smiled at the petite blonde woman who looked up at her over a pair of horn-rimmed glasses.

"How can I help ye?" the woman asked.

"I'd like to be on the next bus to Dublin."

The woman nodded once, then pointed to a sign in the window that listed the fares out of Donegal.

Pepper sighed. She'd been concerned about the cost of the ticket; she was happy to learn she had more than enough in her purse to pay her passage and possibly get something to eat before embarking on the nine-plus-hour bus ride to the Capital.

Pepper handed over the money and was handed in turn a stamped and validated ticket. She thanked the teller and placed the ticket carefully into her handbag beside the mysterious fish's note.

As she turned away from the ticket counter, Pepper noticed a pair of men standing just beyond the corner leading to where the buses had parked. One of them was young, slender, and tall, the other older, stocky, and moustached—and something about them put Pepper's hackles up, although she didn't understand why. Sure, they were looking at her, but that didn't necessarily mean anything; she was standing at the only open ticketing window, and just adjacent to the signage telling passengers all the comings and goings of the buses in and out of the depot. A couple of men looking in her direction shouldn't seem at all out of the ordinary.

But everything about this journey was out of the ordinary. Maybe that was why Pepper felt so uncomfortable under these men's gaze.

She snuck a look back in their direction, they were looking down at something in the younger man's hand—probably a watch. They had probably just been studying the timetable. Pepper felt a little silly. It wasn't like her to be this paranoid. Maybe she was just hungry. Still, something felt wrong and suspicious, and she was technically an international fugitive.

She decided to use their watch-gazing as her cue to leave their line of sight. She'd wanted to go and find a bite to eat anyway. Pepper walked, as quickly as she thought she could while still appearing casual about it, across the open lobby and out onto the sidewalk.

There was just over an hour until the bus was scheduled to leave—that was cutting it close by Irish breakfast standards, but even an abbreviated meal would probably settle her.

Her stomach was growling already—she'd been awake longer than normal for this time of the day, and it was past her usual breakfast time. The little snack she'd packed for the trip had lasted barely half an hour before she'd gobbled it up and had served to do little more than whet her appetite. And since there was every chance her hunger was feeding into her feelings of suspicion and paranoia, breakfast had suddenly gone from a good idea to an outright necessity.

Surely there would be someplace near the station where she could snag a quick bite, maybe even a pastry or two for the road, and also get away from anyone who might or might not be trying to follow her.

It would be worth looking into, anyway.

Pepper pulled her jacket tighter around her as she passed through the exit to the bus terminal. It was much colder in Donegal than she'd expected; the October wind had a bite to it that left her wishing she'd bothered to bring a heavier coat. The little tea rose pinned to her lapel was taking a beating, but its smell carried on the harsh wind as pleasantly as it had on the gentle breezes of Ardara.

She could only hope that was portentous.

Holding her jacket closed with one hand and her hat on her head with the other, Pepper turned her face away from the wind and frowned. She did not want to be out in this weather if she could help it.

Scanning the street through squinted eyes, Pepper spotted a tiny café just on the other side of the street and down to her left. The painted wooden sign hanging out front had blown nearly horizontal on its mountings, but the teapot painted on its front window coupled with a little paper "Open" sign were enough to draw Pepper toward the place.

She stepped off the curb, anxious to get across the street

and into the café's inviting anteroom, and was nearly run over by a speeding lorry approaching from behind her. She lurched backwards, stumbling up the curb as the driver lay on his horn. As he passed, Pepper could see the driver spouting insults in her direction, but between the blaring of the truck's horn and the buffeting of the wind against her ears, Pepper was unable to make out exactly what he was saying.

That was probably for the better.

More than a year in Ireland and she still hadn't grown accustomed to people's driving on the other side of the road. She took a deep breath and looked both ways before venturing out into the street again.

Making her way quickly-but-carefully across the road, Pepper continued to look both ways, and only glanced once over her shoulder at the doors to the bus depot—a thing she immediately wished she hadn't done. Those two men from before were coming through it, scanning the sidewalk up and down as they did.

"Calm down, Pepper," she whispered to herself, "they're probably just hungry—same as you." But she quickened her pace anyway. She figured she wouldn't look too silly hurrying across a street in the same way she might have had she done so across the depot lobby.

Still with one hand on her hat, Pepper arrived at the door to the café. It took a mighty tug to pull it open, and Pepper was more than relieved when she managed to slip through it and into the dimly lit entryway. She stole a quick glance back at the sidewalk and frowned.

Those men were definitely coming this way.

The café was warm. It smelled of fresh bread and peach preserves. Everything about it was a welcome respite from October winds and bus fumes. Pepper took a deep breath and let go of her hat. She straightened her jacket and looked around.

The place was empty save for a plump, white-haired woman sitting just inside the door.

Pepper wondered instantly whether coming into an almost-empty building had been the smart move. If those men really were after her—if they were going to make any trouble for her, it might have been better to have forced any confrontation into someplace crowded and public.

But she'd made her choice and was just going to have to live with it. She smiled at the hostess and moved to un-pin her hat. If those men were about to come in here and accost her, it would be good to have the old woman kindly disposed to her. And if they were coming in for breakfast, she'd do well to finish long before they did and beat a hasty retreat back to the bus station—where she could hide in the ladies restroom until time for her bus to depart.

Hiding in a washroom was about as ignoble a plan as Pepper figured she could come up with, but she was pretty sure it would work. In the meantime, she figured she might as well enjoy the warm and good-smelling place she'd found herself in.

"Sit wherever suits you, dear," the old woman said to Pepper as she rose from her seat to greet her only customer. "Can I bring you a cup of tea?"

"Yes, please," Pepper replied, noticing the eagerness in her own voice as she did. Tea rations had been in very short supply of late—owing to English anger over Irish neutrality. Pepper couldn't remember the last proper cup of tea she'd seen.

Pulling the pin from her hat, Pepper settled on a table by the front window. Looking back out onto the street, Pepper felt a wash of relief come over her as she watched the two men she'd been so nervous of shrug their shoulders and turn back. She let her gaze linger on them as they passed back through the doors of the depot.

They weren't after her. They weren't even after breakfast.

Maybe they'd been looking to meet someone. Or maybe they were looking to have a pint before getting on the road. It was awful early by American standards to drink a beer, but Pepper knew Irish custom to be different regarding such things.

No matter.

They were gone now. She could relax. Still, she was glad for her view of the doors. She'd keep an eye just in case they came back out. Plus, there was a clock on the outside of the bus depot, and she figured it best to keep it in sight.

Whatever that fish had wanted of her, she figured missing her bus wasn't part of the plan.

Chapter 7

"Where'd she go?" Horton McDavish wasn't sure he'd ever been so befuddled by circumstance in his whole life. "She was right there," he insisted, gesturing vaguely at the other side of the street.

Cavill Weathersby sighed in frustration.

It was true. She had been right there just a moment ago. But now, it seemed, she was nowhere at all. Cav withdrew the Compass Rose from his inside coat pocket and opened the hinge. He barely needed to see the mismatched and wobbling petals beneath the glass to know what had happened. Cav looked back at his partner.

This was going to take some explaining.

"She might well still be standing there," Cav said.

Horton harrumphed. She most certainly was not.

"That is quite impossible," he said, stamping his foot as

his hands came to his hips.

"Just as impossible as her being anyplace else without our having seen her leave?" Cav asked incredulously.

Horton's brow furrowed. He didn't have any idea what his partner was on about nor did he particularly care to. All he knew was that this lass they were after had been crossing the road as they'd come out of the building, had taken a few steps along the pavement, turned to face a building, and then somehow gone out of sight. He was sure his eyes were working as well as they always had, so there was no chance she was still standing where she had been. But there was equally no chance she had walked away without his having seen her go.

"You're speaking in riddles," Horton said.

"It's only a riddle to you because you don't understand how these things work," Cav said back.

"To which things are you referring?"

Cav shook his head.

"The talisman," he replied. "We're talking about one of the most powerful arcane items ever known to mankind."

"You're saying this talisman has the power to make a person vanish into thin air?"

"No," Cav replied, "It's..." he looked over at Horton and shook his head again. "You know what?" he offered, "you don't want to hear this."

"I believe you may be correct."

"Come with me," Cav said then, "I have an idea." He turned and headed back toward the bus depot at a clip Horton's much shorter legs had a hard time keeping up with.

"What...?" McDavish began to ask.

"Wherever she is, we've lost the trail," Cav replied before his partner could so much as finish the question. He pulled open the door to the depot wide enough for both of them to pass through it. "There's no use in trying to chase someone we can't see. But...." Cav stopped walking just in front of the ticket window and held up his hand in Horton's direction. He then turned to the lady behind the counter and flashed his most dashing smile. "Top o' the mornin' to ye," he said then, in the most preposterous imitation of an Irish brogue Horton had ever encountered. "I'm wonderin' if you'd be willin' to do me a bit of a favor?"

"What can I hep you with, laddie?" the woman answered.

Horton was a bit agog. He'd seen charming, handsome, young men get their way before, but Cavill Weathersby was on another level. He wasn't sure he'd ever seen his partner told 'no' by anyone. And now here he was currying favors from strange women in Irish bus stations.

"A young lady that was just here," Cav began, "A dark haired lass; she had on a tan suit and a straw cloche hat. Did you sell her a ticket?"

"Yessir, I did."

"Well," Cav began again, his smile growing broader as

he leaned cavalierly against the counter, "would you mind telling me if she's headed to Ardara? I'm nigh on to positive that's the lass my sister shares rooms with, but I don't want to say hello if it turns out she's a stranger. If she's headed to Ardara—that's where my sister lives—I can be closer to sure she is who I think she is."

"Sorry, dear," the woman replied, "I wish I could be of more help, but that young lady is headed to Dublin this morning."

Cavill shrugged dramatically. It was all Horton could do not to roll his eyes.

"Well," Cav said, "I thank you anyway. It was worth a try. You have a nice day now."

"And you too."

Cav patted the counter in front of him as he turned back to his partner. He stepped away from the counter and gestured for Horton to follow.

"So she's headed to Dublin," Cav said, his voice returned to normal, "which means we ought to be headed to Dublin."

"No," Horton argued. "She's got a ticket on the bus to Dublin, which means we ought to be waiting in the bay and catch her when she goes to board."

"Won't work," Cav insisted. "She'll see us and she'll vanish again. We need to get to Dublin ahead of her. We do this right, and she comes to us."

"And how do you suppose we manage that? The next bus

to Dublin is the bus she intends to take—not that I relish the idea of spending any more time aboard a bus to begin with—but there seems to be no way to get to Dublin faster than she will."

"You have no imagination," Cav told him.

"I beg your pardon—"

"We don't need a bus," Cav explained. "We only need to find a phone box. I'll ring Irish Arcanology—I'm sure they'll lend us a car."

"You're sure?" Horton asked, "Irish Arcanology?" Horton had never bothered learning the internal workings of foreign Arcanology desks. Whether or not the Irish had agents on the ground in Donegal was a thing he realized he probably ought to have checked before setting off this morning. But this was Cav's errand, and apparently his young partner had done the necessary legwork.

"Oh, yeah," Cavill answered. "The Irish make the rest of our departments look like children's play. Their ground game is solid, and they've got agents all over the place. And they've mostly forgiven me for poaching Flower from them." Cav grinned as he patted his partner on the shoulder. "They'll get us a car," he assured, "and then we'll get us a girl."

Tea came quickly, in a small ceramic pot with a crocheted yellow cozy around it that appeared to be hand-made. Pepper poured herself a steaming cup, reveling in its warmth and aroma while she examined the menu that had been waiting for her on the table.

Pepper thought it odd that a place this charming, with such good proximity to the bus depot, would be entirely devoid of customers. She quickly chalked it up to the time of day; it was awfully late for breakfast, but not quite truly lunchtime. Surely that was to account for the lack of a crowd.

Pepper decided that had to be the answer. Because if the place was deserted thanks to terrible food or a known vermin problem, she didn't want to know. And if the issue was that it was overpriced, then she didn't really care. She knew how much money she had on her, and she knew how much she'd spent so far. As long as she kept enough in reserve for her return trip to Ardara, she honestly didn't give a damn what happened to the rest.

She decided quickly on a plate of eggs with toast and a grilled tomato, turning her nose up, she hoped not too impolitely, at the day's special of smoked salmon.

If she never saw another salmon again it would be too soon.

The food was everything Pepper had hoped for: hot, tasty, filling, and just fussy enough to keep her focus from wandering too much in the direction of what the hell she was even doing. The pot of tea, although a mite on the weak side, was just enough to last her until the clock at the station said it was time for her to head back across the street. All in all it had been a lovely forty minutes.

And there had been no sign at all of those two men she'd been so creeped out by—a fact which had made her breakfast even more lovely.

The white-haired woman came to clear Pepper's empty dishes from the table, bringing with her the check, which Pepper handed back immediately along with a pair of ten-shilling notes.

Her change was returned only moments later, with a wrapped pastry alongside it.

"For your trip to Dublin, dear," the woman said as she set the sweet down with the pile of coins on the table.

"Thank you," Pepper replied as she stood from her seat, picking up the little parcel and stuffing it into her purse as she did.

The old woman nodded, and Pepper smiled back at her as she re-fastened the button on her jacket and stepped back out onto the chilly Donegal sidewalk.

It wasn't until she was halfway back across the street that it occurred to Pepper she'd never mentioned going to Dublin.

Maybe it wasn't at all strange for the woman to have guessed what she was up to that morning. The café was, after all, just across from a busy bus station with regularly scheduled arrivals and departures. A stranger ordering a large meal at an unusual time of day while keeping a close eye on the depot clock was surely enough to hazard an educated guess on.

Just because weird things were happening, didn't mean everything that happened was weird. Some things were just logical. Still, she decided against looking back at the café as she headed back into the depot...just in case. It was enough to keep an eye out for those two men from before—who seemed, thankfully, to be nowhere about.

Trying her best to ignore the growing warmth of the Labyrinth where it was tucked inside her sleeve, Pepper visited the washroom, then boarded the bus bound for Dublin. In nine hours' time, maybe she'd have some answers.

As the driver pulled the door shut and put the bus into gear, Pepper opened her purse just enough to pull out the little scroll of paper the fish had given her. Nothing new had revealed itself in all the times she'd looked it over, and yet Pepper had been compelled to take it out and puzzle over the thing time and again.

"General McCaslin," she read quietly. Pepper shook her head as she re-rolled the thing and tucked it back into her bag. "Here's hoping you're not a fish."

Chapter 8

I t was dark out when the bus pulled into the Dublin depot. Pepper had forgotten what it was like spending hours in the back of a bus, and she'd begun feeling quite ill less than halfway to their destination. She'd moved seats at that point, finding a spot close to the driver where she could see out both her own window and the vehicle's windscreen. The move had helped a little, as had nibbling on the pastry she'd been given at the café.

But still most of the nine-hour journey had been thoroughly unpleasant. Between her stomach's gurgling and the old bus's craggy suspension, she hadn't been at all sure she would be able to keep her entire breakfast in her stomach for the duration. Add to that the fact that the Labyrinth around her wrist had taken to throbbing between searing hot and icy cold with increasing intensity the closer she grew to her destination, and Pepper was happier than she might have cared to admit when the bus came to a halt.

Careful not to stand too abruptly, Pepper exited the bus as quickly as she could make herself. The air in Dublin was cool, and it felt nice against her face. Hers was the only bus pulled up alongside the station, and now that its engine had been shut off, the diesel fumes had all but cleared. Fresh air was definitely a step in the right direction.

But she had no real idea which direction to go next.

Having never been to Dublin, Pepper had no idea where she was relative to where she was headed.

"That's what I get for taking orders from a salmon," Pepper mumbled as she headed toward the depot building. Her fellow passengers had gone inside already; that seemed to be the logical next step. Standing outside alone in the dark certainly wasn't doing her any favors.

From the side she'd entered, the bus depot had looked like a rather abbreviated affair, with modern lines and too many windows. But one step inside the door was enough to tell Pepper the place was quite the opposite. The bus area had just been tucked in an inauspicious corner.

The station, Pepper learned from a giant placard above the door, was in Amiens Street and from the looks of it might have been the central transportation hub for the entire city. While scanning over the signs "To Trains", "To City Buses," and "To Taxis," Pepper managed to spot a large map mounted behind glass on the far wall.

She scurried across the yellow linoleum toward it.

Starting at the *You Are Here* marker on the map, she combed over the thing intensely, making concentric circles with her finger as she read every mark in search of her destination. She could only hope she'd find it on this map. The address was Dublin 2, which told Pepper it ought to be in the city proper, and not some suburb. But there was still a chance it was too small a street to show on the map.

She was beginning to get nervous that she wouldn't find it when her eyes landed squarely on the words "Temple Bar". Pepper took a deep breath and sighed.

There it was.

Not only had she found Temple Bar, but it wasn't terribly far away. It wasn't much farther a walk than Ardara was from her cottage—probably just under twenty minutes. That was a distance easily managed in a city, even after dark. Pepper was grateful for that small fortune. She'd rather not have spent money on a taxi and the thought of having to take another bus didn't sit well with her at the moment. She was quite happy that she wouldn't need to. She felt almost relaxed as she repeated the directions over and over again in her head. She made a simple melody of them, so she'd be more likely to remember, and she sang softly to herself as she headed for the door.

She jumped at the sound of a car starting just outside;

her whole body started and she slapped her hand against her chest. How lost in thought had she just been? Apparently she'd let herself get too relaxed—relaxed enough that the ordinary sounds of the city had the ability to startle and frighten her.

"Well, that was ridiculous," Pepper said to herself, shaking her head as she caught her breath. "It's a car, not a dragon."

The car's headlights streamed across her path and Pepper made an effort not to pay them any mind. She wasn't sure why she was so on edge; it was probably an artifact of having been forced to sit still for so long coupled with a not-insignificant degree of hunger and thirst.

And she still couldn't shake the feeling from back in Donegal that she was being followed. Telling herself once again that idea made absolutely no sense, Pepper turned her attention back to the task at hand. She hadn't come all this way to get waylaid in a car park.

As Pepper started toward Temple Bar, once again quietly singing the directions to herself, she couldn't help but take note of how pleasant the weather seemed. It was a good bit warmer in Dublin than it had been in Donegal and Ardara, but not so warm as to make her want to take off her jacket. The air had felt cool and refreshing against her skin after the stifling conditions of a long bus ride, and she was pleased at how mild the night air was in the city.

It would be a lovely night for walking.

Dublin was a bigger city than Pepper had imagined it. Even after dark it was a bustling metropolis with traffic at every light and smartly-dressed pedestrians hurrying to get wherever fashionable Irish folk went in the evenings. It felt a little like Seattle, save for how gentle and easily navigable the city's few hills were, and for a moment Pepper was homesick.

She wondered what life was like in Washington these days. She'd gotten what little information she could about America from reading papers and watching newsreels, but the conditions in the Pacific Northwest never seemed to be addressed specifically. What was coffee and sugar rationing doing to her father's temperament? Did milk rationing also apply to families with cows of their own? What was it like living under the Blackout Rules?

Would she even recognize Seattle as the place she'd left? She'd taken off so early into American involvement in the war that most of the wartime privation hadn't hit her hometown yet. She wished she could know how much harder things had gotten since she'd gone.

She wished she could just call home and make sure everyone was coping.

But she couldn't let herself get lost in her feelings—because that could very easily lead to her getting lost in a foreign city. Pepper had never been particularly good at urban orienteering and she needed to pay keen attention to where she was and which way to turn if she wanted to end up at her intended destination.

She knew the difficult part was over when she spotted the river Liffey at the end of the block she'd just turned onto. The river was a pretty major landmark, an indication she was getting close to the end of her journey.

Journey to *where* and *why* were still questions that were very much burning in her mind, but at least she could be confident that she was headed in the right direction. Temple Bar was just across that river and down a ways. She was close.

She was thankful the end of her walk was nearing. Her curiosity had been piqued all the way back in Ardara, and she was getting more and more excited to learn just what she'd been summoned for. But more than that, her hackles were up.

She was sure she'd been spotting the same black car just behind her the whole time she'd been walking. Her more suspicious nature could have convinced her it was the same car she'd been so startled by back at the bus station, and the most paranoid part of her brain might even suspect the occupants were the two men she'd thought were tailing her back in Donegal.

Of course, this made absolutely no practical sense.

No one was after her. No one even knew she was here.

And of course it looked like the same car. They all looked like the same car. There wasn't a whole lot of automotive variety in Ireland to begin with, and in the darkness it was impossible to tell the difference between their various dark-colored paint jobs.

She was in a strange city, on a strange errand, and it had her feeling apprehensive. That made sense—far more sense than any suspicion that she was being pursued.

Still, when she looked toward the river and saw the nearest bridge was foot-traffic only, she felt a tinge of relief. Men in an automobile couldn't tail her across a footbridge. And even though her rational brain was still telling her there was no way she was actually being followed, her gut still said this bridge was a welcome escape.

The white iron footbridge was a pretty thing, at the same time both formal and inviting with its tall scrollwork arches topped with glowing golden lamps. Its deck was an easy slope and the breeze off the river wasn't at all uncomfortable—just enough to bring the smell of the rose in Pepper's lapel wafting over the native aromas of the city. The Labyrinth had settled into a pleasant pulsing against her wrist; that had to be portentous.

Right?

She made her way across the footbridge and carefully counted streets as she walked the few additional blocks past the river until she came to the street marker for Temple Bar. Pepper paused then. She withdrew the scroll from her purse again and read it over.

"Number twenty-A," she read aloud to herself, as though

she hadn't had the address committed to memory since long before she'd set out from Ardara this morning.

Pepper looked back and forth along the street ahead of her. The streetlights were dim, but this was clearly a business row, and enough of the shingles and doorways had visible numbers marking their addresses.

She turned left. Number Twenty-A should be within a block.

She made her way quickly down the street, all the sudden in a great hurry to get where she was going. The Labyrinth's pulsing had grown faster, more intense, and had her own pulse racing in time. And clouds had begun to gather overhead, threatening a downpour that Pepper would just as soon not be caught out in.

Pepper charged down the crowded sidewalk, counting out loud as she read the numbers on the businesses to her left and right. A pub at Number Eighteen extended into Nineteen, and a restaurant at number Twenty continued into Twenty-One.

Twenty-Two. And Twenty-Three. And then came the end of the block. A gust of wind caught Pepper's skirt just as she felt the first raindrop fall onto her shoulder.

Pepper stopped in the street and stamped her foot. This could not be happening. How—how in the name of all things arcane could she have been sent across the country, through wind and cold and diesel fumes and now rain, only to find that number Twenty-A didn't exist.

She turned around and walked past the two addresses again.

She hadn't been wrong. Number Twenty was adjacent to number Twenty-One and both of them were assigned to a pub called Gallagher's. The Labyrinth had grown oddly dormant, and the rain was picking up. This was beginning to look like even more of a fool's errand than she'd initially figured it to be.

What kind of insane leprechaun chase had she been sent on? She considered turning back, but she just couldn't make herself walk away. Maybe it was her scholarly curiosity, or maybe her natural stubbornness was behind it, but she knew deep down she wasn't leaving this street until she had this mystery solved.

"Dammit!"

Pepper shook her head and walked back to stand in front of the painted brick pillar that seemed to be the only thing separating the two numbered areas. She reached into her bag and pulled out the scroll again, hunching her shoulders to shield it from the falling rain.

The words had vanished. In their place was a portrait of a dragon. It looked pencil-drawn, although in impossibly fine detail for its size.

"What the hell?" she screamed, looking back and forth between the scroll and the building. The Labyrinth flared ice cold against her skin and then went dormant again.

And then she saw it.

Tiny and brass, in a script that might have looked at first glance like no more than decorative scrollwork, the number Twenty-A was affixed to the bricks directly in front of her. Keeping her eyes fixed on the tiny marker, Pepper stepped toward it.

It grew larger.

Another step, larger still. And another, and another, until the characters had grown to normal height and beneath them had appeared a door she was quite certain hadn't been there previously.

Or, rather, it hadn't been visible previously. Pepper had come to know just enough about magical things to know she shouldn't take for granted what was and was not present. A person's eyes could deceive them.

Either way, it didn't matter. The door was here and it was visible and the Labyrinth had once again grown icy cold. This was the place.

The door was an old thing—brittle-looking and shoddily put together from what Pepper could tell. It might once have been painted black; its chipped, peeling, and sun-bleached paint reminded Pepper of the skin of a molting reptile. When she took hold of its handle, the sounds in the street vanished from her perception. The raindrops ceased. The Labyrinth flared warm. And the door, now in full relief, filled her entire field of view.

It was bolted in three places.

The door was flanked by a pair of narrow windows, each hung with tattered velvet curtains that had escaped their rings in several places. The interior seemed completely dark and abandoned. Even when she pressed her face against the glass, Pepper was unable to see anything inside. She stood back and glowered.

This was the place.

And since when had a locked door ever stopped Pepper Elizabeth Jones?

Chapter 9

Once, when Pepper was eleven years old, the shed where her family kept the garden tools had been burgled. Pepper had discovered this when she'd gone to the shed to fetch the hedge clippers for her mother. She remembered the confusion she'd felt when she'd slid open the shed's tin door to find its contents had all seemed to vanish. That feeling of dissonance and disbelief in what she was seeing had stuck with her ever since.

And this feeling was a super-powered reprise of that feeling.

The room she stepped into was not at all what Pepper had presumed awaited her on the other side of that decrepit-looking door. In fact, it couldn't have been more the opposite. It was a large room, much larger than the exterior would have allowed a person to guess. Just as oddly, the ample room was brightly lit, dotted with wooden tables, and seemingly bursting with merriment.

Smells of warm bread, sweet whiskey and vanilla wafted through the air, finally laying to rest Pepper's earlier feeling of nausea and replacing it with a powerful hunger.

The right-hand wall was dominated by a large oak bar, at which men in outdated but still smart-looking evening suits sat upon leather stools sipping brandy from oversized snifters. A fireplace dominated the far wall, a low and inviting flame crackling within it. A fiddle and bodhran band played a lively tune from atop a makeshift stage fashioned out of lashed-together crates that stood in the center of the room. Women in heavy skirts with soot-marked faces danced gleefully around them while a group of children watched, occasionally attempting to mimic a step.

There were men and women dressed in formalwear of a bygone era clinking glasses just beyond the bar, and a troop of what appeared to be Black American Union soldiers playing cards by the fire. A man dressed in rags sat in a corner reading a leatherbound book.

Pepper had to wonder whether she had perhaps intruded on some sort of costume party. It was October, after all, and Halloween was known to be a heartily-celebrated occasion in Ireland. That would surely be an explanation for the patrons' unexpected and widely disparate manners of dress, not to mention the wide range of ethnicities, from every corner of the globe.

All present seemed to have a drink in hand.

It wasn't a moment before a blonde-haired lad with strangely pointed ears approached Pepper and slid a pint of ale into her hand.

"Thanks," Pepper said, "what do I...?" but before she was able to finish her sentence, the fellow had gone, disappearing into a crowd of merrymakers trading toasts around one of the larger tables by the bar.

A pair of young girls were running toward Pepper—hand in hand, they dashed across the room, dodging the dancing girls and frolicking folk with athletic precision. Identical save for their coloring, the two appeared to be school age—eight, or maybe nine, Pepper figured. They came to a sudden halt directly in front of Pepper and looked her squarely in the eye.

The twin on Pepper's left was perhaps the palest human she'd ever seen. With white-blonde hair, alabaster skin, and eyes that were only barely blue, she looked unreal—almost other-worldly as she gazed somberly up at Pepper. In stark contrast stood the twin to Pepper's left. Her hair was a fiery golden copper, her eyes a vibrant green-blue, and her rosy cheeks were dotted with tiny freckles. Pepper couldn't help the thought that if the two could just have been averaged together, they'd make a perfectly unremarkable pair.

The colorful twin shot Pepper a most pleasant smile as she reached up and slapped the flagon of ale out of her hand.

The pale twin had no reaction at all.

"Faireen says not to drink that," the brightly colored girl said.

"Who's Faireen?" Pepper asked in, frowning at the puddle of ale on the floor at her feet.

The girl snorted, rolling her eyes as she inclined her head toward the paler twin.

"I'm Peg," she said, "that's Faireen. She won't talk to you. She only talks to me."

"Of course," Pepper muttered as the twins let go of each other and each took hold of one of her hands instead. They led her through the room, past a table full of boisterous American sailors and a circle of Japanese schoolchildren playing a game with beanbags on the floor.

"Why shouldn't I drink it?" Pepper asked as she stumbled along behind the two insistent children.

"You can't drink anything here," Peg answered. Not missing a step, she shook her head and continued. "And you can't eat anything either. Accepting any hospitality here means you're trapped here forever. And we can't have that now, can we?"

Pepper shook her head and sighed. A pint of ale would likely have done her good. She was hungry and thirsty to the point of feeling a little grumpy at being manhandled by a pair of children in a pub.

"Where are we going?" Pepper asked as the twins led

her through the throng of dancing girls, past the makeshift stage, and toward the fireplace.

"You're here for the Dragon, aren't you? We're taking you to see General McCaslin."

The bunch of them stopped in front of the fireplace and Faireen gestured to the flames on her sister's side.

"Huh?" Pepper asked. On the one hand, she was a bit relieved to hear the name that had been written on the scroll when she'd found it in the salmon, but on the other hand she was getting more and more nervous about what dragons had to do with any of this.

She turned and glowered at the children.

Faireen glowered in return. Her expression darkened and she pointed menacingly into the crackling flames.

Pepper took a deep breath and looked down at the Labyrinth. It had come loose from her sleeve and now dangled visibly from her wrist. She took hold of it with her opposite hand, trying to get any sense at all of its current temperature.

But there was nothing.

Still, somehow this felt like a portentous moment. There was magic in this place, she was sure of it. And in a place so obviously full of magic, it would do her well not to defy the wishes of a creepy child issuing silent orders.

But walking into a fireplace was not an idea that appealed to her. She pursed her lips and took another step toward the hearth. Out of the corner of her eye, Pepper could see Peg cross her arms over her chest and shake her head in clear annoyance.

Having no idea what she was supposed to do next, Pepper shook her head as well. She looked deeper into the stone fireplace, casting her gaze into the flames with as much intensity as she could summon. She rather hoped she looked like a serious caster working a spell, but figured her affect wasn't doing much to mask her confusion.

"You're not even looking," Peg chided.

"I don't know what I'm supposed to be looking for!" Pepper insisted, turning back to face the two children.

Faireen was still pointing into the fireplace. Frowning, Peg now pointed as well.

Pepper threw up her hands, but turned again to face the fireplace, this time forcing her gaze to follow precisely the trajectory of the little girls' fingers as she drew still closer to the hearth.

It took a moment for Pepper to notice the fireplace was much deeper than it appeared from even a few feet away. The chimney opened up wide immediately past the mantle, allowing ample room for a person to stand inside the fireplace.

Tentatively, Pepper ducked beneath the mantle.

The heat from the fire was intense, but not uncomfortable, and the smoke off the logs was barely noticeable. Pepper looked to her right: in the direction she could only guess the two girls were still pointing.

There was a doorway in the side of the fireplace.

Pepper swallowed hard. She wanted to close her eyes, but figured that would be a very bad idea when stepping directly into a burning fireplace. As quickly as she could while still being sure of her footing, she stepped into the space beside the fire and pushed open the door.

The passageway on the other side was dark, particularly so as Pepper's own shadow blocked out what little light from the fire spilled around its first abrupt corner. Her foot found a stair, and then another. She credited a childhood spent exploring the rocky Washington shoreline for her ability to keep her balance, despite her eyes not having time to adjust.

With one hand on the cool stone wall, Pepper made her way down the tight spiral of shallow stone stairs. The walk felt interminable—these stairs seemed to stretch downward forever, and Pepper couldn't help the thought that she was not going to enjoy the trip back up.

Just when she was beginning to wonder if she would ever reach the bottom, a slant of dim light eked its way into Pepper's periphery. She quickened her pace down the stairs as the light grew greater and brighter, until she could easily see the steps beneath her shoes and the curved walls on either side of her. The walls on either side were scarcely wider than her shoulders, giving Pepper a slight feeling of claustrophobia; for a moment she missed the blissful ignorance of not being able to see how cramped and narrow the passage was.

But she continued downward—not that there would likely have been enough room to turn around even if she'd cared to try. She took pains to steady her breath, calming herself as best she could as she focused on the ever-increasing light ahead.

Very abruptly at the end of the staircase stood a heavy wooden door. It was rounded at the top, with a giant iron knocker in the shape of a Dragon's head, and a keyhole large enough that Pepper could have fit her whole hand inside.

It looked like something out of a storybook. The door struck Pepper as something ancient, yet nothing about it looked to be at all aged or in disrepair. The iron handle and hinges were all oiled and shiny and the wood was smooth and evenly stained.

There was a non-zero chance there could be a dragon on the other side of this door. Pepper wasn't sure how she felt about that, and the Labyrinth, still dormant at her wrist, was being no help. Still, she'd come this far; she might as well keep going.

Unless, of course, she came face-to-face with a dragon, then she would absolutely turn and run.

Pepper reached for the knocker.

Just as her fingers first brushed the iron loop in the dragon's mouth, the door swung gently open, revealing the room beyond. For a moment, Pepper had to shield her eyes; the room was garishly, fluorescently bright—an uncomfortable contrast to the darkness in the stairwell. She'd only thought her eyes had failed to adjust.

Pepper moved tentatively into the room beyond, pleased with the fact there was no dragon in evidence. She hadn't thought there would really be a dragon living beneath the pub, but she hadn't *not* thought that either. It was a relief to see there was no such thing.

The room she stepped into was as chaotic as the one above it, but with none of its attendant frivolity. Instead of upbeat music, the room echoed with wails and cries. In the place of frolicking dancers and playful children were dozens—hundreds maybe—of men and women huddled and shaking, taking up every available space on the furniture and floor. They leaned against each other. Some stared blankly at the walls or into space. A few were looking around the room, their eyes searching the crowd.

The men wore suits and ties, but not in a fashion Pepper had ever seen before. Many of the women wore suits as well, some with trousers and blouses that resembled undergarments to her eyes. Hairstyles and cosmetics all seemed odd and off-putting. There was something distinctly out-of-sorts about the lot of them.

Some were marred with burns, many covered in dust. All appeared recently traumatized. More than one of them held a small device in their hand: a military radio, maybe, or miniature adding machine. They poked and punched at what looked like numerical keyboards, occasionally extending an antenna or holding the gadget above their head while looking expectantly at it. Whatever these things were, they seemed to be of particular value.

But Pepper couldn't allow herself to be distracted by the presence of unfamiliar gizmos. She was here for a reason, and anything confounding her ability to find this General McCaslin person and figure out just why a fish had sent her to this bizarre locale was a distraction she just didn't need.

She looked around, trying to pick out anyone who might be the General, but there were no men in uniform of any rank that she could identify.

So there was no General in evidence, but there was no dragon either—so at least there was that.

The only standout in the room was a woman. She was stout, maybe around Pepper's age—but possibly much older —and had a look on her face like nothing going on in this room was at all unusual or off-putting. She was dressed in a long skirt with an old-fashioned shirtwaist that was coming untucked in places. Her hair was a dark ginger color and upon it was pinned a flower-crested pancake hat. A ribbon hung down around her skirts from where it attached at her waist; Pepper's guess was it had been meant to drape over her opposite shoulder.

The woman, although seemingly unbothered by whatever had everyone else so troubled, was moving through the room with purpose. A basket in one hand and a roll of bandages in the other, she saw to one person and then the next—dressing wounds and soothing cries as she went. All the while her tone was soft and her manner calm.

Pepper found herself a little bit mesmerized. She wasn't sure how long she'd been gaping when the woman looked up at her and frowned.

"And you are?" she asked, casting a pointed scowl in Pepper's direction.

"I'm Pepper Jones."

"Can I help you, Pepper Jones?" The woman answered in what might have been the thickest brogue Pepper had ever heard. Her tone seemed impatient—in great contrast to the way she'd been speaking just a moment before. It occurred to Pepper that introduction had been a bit lacking in necessary information.

"I'm looking for a General McCaslin," she replied. "I was led to believe he'd be here."

"Aye!" the woman called back. She looked away then and moved on to continue her ministrations, setting her basket on the floor beside a trembling woman with wide eyes and ashes in her hair. "I'm the General ye be seekin'. And if it isn't too obvious, I'm a mite occupied at the moment." She gestured to the crowd of weeping and injured people all around her. "Make yourself useful, Pepper Jones," she said then "Can't you see there's been a disaster?"

General McCaslin gestured to a wooden bucket just to the right of where Pepper stood. It was halfway filled with water, and a dented metal ladle hung over the side.

Pepper nodded. She understood.

Sort of.

She understood that she'd just found, and perhaps just offended, the general to whom the letter in the fish's mouth had sent her. She understood that there was magic at work in this place and she understood that it would likely behoove her greatly to be as helpful as possible in this situation.

She still did not understand where she was or what she was doing here. And she had no idea what any of it had to do with any dragons.

She'd been warned only in the broadest terms what taking hold of the Labyrinth would mean for her life moving forward. This moment had her pretty well convinced she was farther out of her depth than she'd ever been in her life.

A lot was happening that Pepper had no real clue about. But she knew how to carry a pail of water.

Pepper moved to lift the bucket by its handle, bracing herself for the weight of the water inside, but found the thing to be oddly light and manageable. Starting with the pair of men the General had just left, she began to make her way around the room, offering ladles full of water to anyone who cared to have a drink, careful to give the bustling General McCaslin as wide a berth as possible.

Somehow Pepper was unsurprised at the fact the bucket in her hands seemed to be bottomless. It remained as full as it had been at first glance even after everyone had drunk their fill.

Gently then, but with a power of magical suggestion that even Pepper could feel, General McCaslin herded the men and women onto their feet and up the stairs. Slowly but surely, they all filed past Pepper and into the stairwell, until only she and the General remained.

General McCaslin took a deep breath and mopped at her brow with her sleeve. She plopped down to sit on a stray bench in the middle of the room. When she looked up, she seemed surprised to see Pepper still standing in the corner.

"Who are you, again?" she asked, removing a handkerchief from her skirt pocket and beginning to blot at her chest where her blouse had come open.

"Pepper Jones."

"Aye," the General answered with a frown. "Pepper Jones. What I meant to ask ye then was what you're doin' in my line of sight."

"I can't say I rightly know," Pepper answered her honestly. "I was rather hoping you could tell me. You see, I found a piece of paper in a fish's mouth and it said to come to an address and to find you and then two little children upstairs wouldn't let me eat or drink anything and they showed me to the stairs in the fireplace and now, I guess, here you are, and here I am, and I guess there's something about a dragon. And I truly have no idea."

General McCaslin shook her head as she stood and took a step in Pepper's direction.

"'M afraid I'm going to need a bit more than that," she replied. "Could ya at least tell me when you got this note from a fish?"

"Just yesterday morning," Pepper replied, "I'd gone to the fishmonger's like I do almost every day and…"

"No," General McCaslin interrupted, "not that when. What was the date?" she asked. "Month and year. If you please."

"It's October of 1943."

General McCaslin visibly balked. She ran her hands through the mess of fallen hair at her temples and frowned pointedly at Pepper where she stood. Pepper knew that look of disapproval, and she didn't like it. She had no idea why this disheveled woman in an out-of-date dress would look at her so angrily, but she was about ready to give this General a real what for.

Who had summoned whom after all?

"I'd tell you you're not what I expected, Pepper Jones," the General told her, "but I'm not good at subtlety and you can probably see it clear across my face. So what I'll say instead is that I'm often underestimated myself and so I'll take it on faith that you're who I need."

The General looked Pepper up and down, sizing her up the way a person might a fine cut of meat. Pepper tried not to squirm, but the scrutiny was palpable. The General's gaze lingered at Pepper's wrist, her eyebrows lifted, and she grinned and nodded her head.

"Indeed," she said quietly, "it is you."

"I appreciate your faith in me, ma'am," Pepper said back, setting down the pail of water, "but would you mind backing up a little?"

"What do you mean, backing up?" the General asked, "what is it you think you need?"

"Well, for starters," Pepper answered, "you just said you need me. Need me for what, exactly? All I had was an address in a fish's mouth—and even that vanished when I got to the door. Nobody's told me anything about why I'm here. If you wouldn't mind, please: what is all this? And what does it have to do with a dragon? Because if I'm expected to slay one..."

Her sentence was interrupted by the General's laughter.

Pepper balled her hands into fists before slamming them onto her hips. She didn't appreciate being laughed at.

"You think this is funny?"

General McCaslin shook her head as she crossed her arms over her chest. She continued to laugh softly as she sank into a seat on top of an upturned bucket.

"Well now I see why it's you," General McCaslin said, her voice suddenly warm and comforting. She quirked her lip and laughed again, softly this time, before looking Pepper square on. "Come have a seat, Pepper Jones," she beckoned, "'cause what I'm about to tell ye is gonna blow your mind."

The sting of being laughed at had begun to fade, so Pepper did as she was asked, moving to sit on an empty stool near where the General had stationed herself. She took a deep breath, noticing as she went to sit just how unsteady she was.

"Am I about to be asked to slay a dragon?" she asked.

"You really have no idea what's going on here?" General McCaslin leaned forward to rest her elbows on her knees.

"Really," Pepper assured her, "no idea."

"I can promise you no dragons to be slain," General McCaslin assured her, "but brace yourself, Pepper Jones. Because we're going to need you to save magic."

Chapter 10

Pepper swallowed hard, absently fingering the labyrinth where it hung from her wrist as she looked up at the General.

"You want me to...?" Pepper hardly recognized her own voice. Somehow this was even more concerning than the idea of having to slay a dragon.

"There's a cult," McCaslin said then, nodding her head once as she moved to stand, "headquartered in the Black Forest."

Pepper shuddered.

"A cult," she repeated.

"Aye," the General said. She shook her head as she began to pace. "The once-laughable Thule Gesellschaft has joined forces with the Vril society. That combination of unbridled hatred and focused energy may just be enough to do this terrible thing."

"A terrible thing?"

"The most terrible," the General replied. "There is a ritual planned that could very well lead to them having full control over all the world's arcane energy. If they succeed, it will change the tide of the war and the direction of history. They cannot be allowed to succeed."

The urgency in the General's voice was unmistakable; Pepper's palms began to sweat as she listened.

"The Black Forest," Pepper said. She hadn't understood much of what the McCaslin had just told her, but one particular piece of this puzzle had fallen alarmingly into place. She wasn't going to be able to think about anything else. "That's in Germany."

"Aye," the General affirmed. "It is."

"Nazi Germany!"

"For the next thousand years if they have any say in the matter." The General looked nonplussed, but the force of her words punched Pepper right in the gut.

"What the hell do you expect me to do?" Pepper asked, trying not to let her abject terror at the idea she may be sent to fight Nazis get to her, "Parachute behind enemy lines?"

Suddenly the idea of maybe being sent to slay a dragon sounded like a really great idea.

General McCaslin glowered, casting her gaze down at the Labyrinth where it hung from Pepper's wrist.

"Did ya think that came without obligation?" she asked.

"Oh...." Pepper swallowed hard. She realized she'd been unconsciously tapping her toe—she wasn't sure just how long she'd been at it, but a cramp in her ankle told her it had been more than a moment. She took the Labyrinth between her thumb and forefinger and nodded.

"Oh," the General repeated. There was less mocking in her tone than Pepper hoped to credit her with, and somehow she managed not to take offense.

"I have to do this," she said softly.

"There's nobody forcing you."

"You are."

"I tell you I'm not. I'm not in a position to force your hand, Pepper Jones."

"How come that doesn't make me feel any better?"

"Likely because you're beginning to understand. Someone's got to do it—and, for whatever reason, you've been chosen for the task."

"Why me?" Pepper shrugged and stood from her seat, shaking her head as she began to pace. This was big. Too Big. Far bigger than anything she was prepared to take on, and The General's assurance she'd been somehow chosen to take it on wasn't inspiring any confidence.

"Now there's a question we've all asked a time or three," General McCaslin replied.

"So you can't tell me."

"Your guess is as good as mine."

Pepper stopped her pacing and took a deep breath. Something in her gut was telling her the General knew more than she was sharing. But that didn't make sense, did it? Why would somebody obfuscate when they were trying to talk a person into a dangerous thing?

To hide how dangerous the thing is.

Pepper answered her own question. But it wasn't helping. Her gut was telling her saying no wasn't an option.

"He'd have done it, wouldn't he?" she asked quietly, as much to herself as to General McCaslin.

"I've no idea to whom you're referring."

"The man who left me with this." Pepper held up her arm and looked down at the Labyrinth where it hung. "He'd have done it. He'd have marched right in and fought the Nazis. And he'd have beaten them," she declared frankly, "or died trying."

Mr. Miyamoto would have done everything he could. Pepper knew that because she'd seen it. When she'd agreed to go to work at Camp Harmony, she hadn't seen the place for the atrocity it was—but Mr. Miyamoto had changed that. He'd shown her the horror of her own government's policies and he'd shown her a way forward she could never have imagined on her own.

The way he'd railed against what America was putting his people through had been nothing short of heroic, and the way he'd committed himself—right up to the moment of his death—to keeping the Labyrinth and all it contained safe and well-tended had shown Pepper what lengths she might be asked to go to for the same.

She just hadn't imagined she'd be asked for so much so soon.

"They put him in a camp," Pepper said, sinking back into her seat. "Just because he was Japanese. The Americans—my own country—they're supposed to be the good guys. But they're putting innocent people into camps. Mr. Miyamoto fought back. He got out—and I went with him. He died to get this back." Pepper held up her wrist, dangling the Labyrinth between them for emphasis. "He died for it—and he gave it to me. He'd fight the Nazis," she declared, "and he'd expect me to do the same."

"I believe you may be right," the General said.

"It's appalling," Pepper said, "what America's doing."

"And the Germans?"

"They're worse," Pepper answered, "A lot worse."

"Do you say that because you believe it truly, or because you're an American and that's the way you're supposed to feel?"

Pepper squirmed in her seat. She honestly wasn't sure. She'd heard from her father and others for years now how wicked and racist and awful Chancellor Hitler and his policies were. But America's atrocities, she'd seen up close. Could she even judge one against the other? Could she be sure at this distance whose wrongs were the greater? Was it even her place to make such judgments?

"I don't think that really matters," she answered after a moment. It was a rare flash of clarity, but there it was all the same.

"You don't?"

"I don't," Pepper affirmed. "What Germany is doing is wrong," she stated plainly, "whether or not that's more wrong than what America is doing isn't really up to me to decide. What is up to me to decide is whether I'm willing to try and fight the wrong—and I made that choice back at Camp Harmony. I should do the right thing. And if that means storming into Nazi Germany, then..."

"It won't be so much as storming," General McCaslin corrected her.

"Sneaking, then," Pepper allowed. "If it means I have to sneak myself into Nazi Germany, then I think that's what I ought to do."

General McCaslin smiled—it was a self-satisfied, inhumanly wide grin. Pepper found it frightening; she couldn't help herself but to shudder visibly.

"Very well then," the General said after a beat. "You'll leave this building as you arrived: up the stairs and out through the crowd. Careful still not to eat or drink while inside these walls. Out and to the left then, a left again at the streetlight.

Another left at the river, then right across the bridge. And you must not look back as you cross! There you'll meet a car. Its driver will take you to the next stop—where you'll meet..." the General paused to consider her words.

Pepper steeled herself—if the word 'dragon' was about to be spoken, she didn't want to react too visibly.

"...an associate of mine," General McCaslin settled on a turn of phrase. "She's waiting already. She'll tell you what comes next."

"Um... okay," Pepper said, standing up as she nodded. She did her best not to let the level of effort she was making to remember those instructions show on her face. Nor her unease at the idea that this 'associate' could still be a dragon. "That's it?" she asked. "That's all?"

"Not all," McCaslin replied. Her expression grew dark and her bearing suddenly felt menacing. Pepper tried, and failed, not to appear as frightened as she was.

"What else?" she asked. It was taking every bit of will she had not to creep backwards as the General began to close the distance between them.

"At the center of the rite these Nazis wish to perform, there is a stone," she replied, her voice growing gravelly and her nostrils beginning to flare. "A gem," she clarified, "An item of unspeakable power—for those who know how to wield it." The General ceased her forward progress and balled her hands into fists as she continued. "The foolish beings who allowed it to fall into Nazi hands were comforted by the notion that none among their ranks would possess that knowledge; how very wrong they were." The General took another step forward, looking Pepper squarely in the eye. "You are to bring me that stone," she said. "Take it from them and bring it here—where they will never find it—where they will never be able to get it back. Bring it to me," she said again, "and save the world."

Pepper swallowed hard, trying her best to ignore the fact that she was very sure the General's eyes had, for a moment, glowed a scarlet red at the center. She nodded her understanding.

"Okay," she managed to say after a moment.

General McCaslin smiled then, it was the same easy smile she'd worn earlier—as though all the intensity of the previous moment had evaporated.

"Okay," she affirmed, her voice having also returned to its normal tambor. "That's it, then. You're to go behind enemy lines, find the gem, bring it back to me, and save the future of magic. Are you sure you're up to the task?"

Pepper squared her shoulders and set her jaw.

"Yes ma'am," she replied, trying to sound the way she imagined a person should sound when replying to a General. As she turned to head back toward the stairs that led up to the fireplace, Pepper could only hope the General hadn't been able to tell she was lying.

Chapter 11

The sun had long since set when Pepper had arrived at number Twenty-A Temple Bar, but somehow the night had grown still darker while she'd been inside. Perhaps it was an eccentricity of the streetlights, or maybe just a trick of her own eyes, but as Pepper stepped through the door from the tavern and onto the street, the amplified darkness felt ominous and creepy.

Pepper Jones did not like it one bit.

She resolved to get to her next destination in a hurry.

As the door clicked shut behind her, Pepper had to fight the urge to turn and look back at it. She wondered if the mysterious address would look as dim and deserted now as it had when she'd first managed to see it, or if maybe it had already vanished back into the bricks between the windows of numbers Twenty and Twenty-One.

But General McCaslin had told her not to look back. The edict had referred specifically to the bridge across the Liffey, but even Pepper's limited experience with arcane matters of this import had been enough to tell her there was no such thing as being too careful. She did her best to tamp down her curiosity as she stepped away from the building and out onto the crowded sidewalk.

All around her, Temple Bar was a thriving, vibrant neighborhood. If anyone had found her entrée onto the street peculiar, they surely weren't bothered enough to stop and speak of it. People were coming and going in all directions, none of them paying Pepper any mind; some of them passing oddly close not to offer at least a nod in acknowledgement. That felt creepy, too.

"To the left and then left again," Pepper whispered to herself as she began walking. If memory served her she was being sent back just the way she came. That was good. She knew which way she'd come and she'd be better able to keep up her hurried pace without having to stop and read the street signs.

That was, if she was really back in Dublin.

Because there was every chance the door to number Twenty-A had been a door to someplace else entirely.

If, instead of an ordinary (albeit peculiar) tavern, the place she'd just visited was a faerie knowe—existing outside the world as she understood it—that would go a long way in accounting for the oddities she'd seen within. Hadn't she heard in a story somewhere not to accept the hospitality of faeries?

The farther she got from the tavern—from the strangely-dressed disaster victims, the General in the basement, the odd children, and talk of dragons—the sillier she felt about the idea.

What was the thing her father had always said? The simplest explanation was usually correct?

But, the more thought she gave to the matter, it became clearer and clearer that the simplest explanation wasn't the mundane one.

Pepper Jones had just visited a place very much outside of reality.

And maybe she hadn't altogether left that place.

The city seemed different as she made her way back down the street toward the river. And it wasn't just that the night had grown darker than before—although that continued to creep her out a bit.

The sky had cleared. All hints of an oncoming storm had dissipated, leaving an ink-black sky mottled with more stars than Pepper was used to seeing in a city. And the temperature had gone up—odd for an Irish October night. The chill had left the air entirely.

It was a perfectly fine night for walking.

But still the world around Pepper felt somehow...

unnatural.

The air was calm; the wind off the river, so blustery when she'd arrived in the street, was now barely more than a gentle breeze bringing the scent of tea rose from her lapel to her nostrils.

Mismatched gas and electric lamps appeared to be glowing in an identical hue. Music and chatter still spilled onto the sidewalks from open pub doors and revelers on the street, but their sounds were muffled, reminding Pepper of what her radio sounded like when she had her ears bundled up in her favorite wool blanket.

Things were peculiar, but not unpleasant.

If she hadn't been on an ominous errand, headed for Nazi Germany at the behest of a peculiar General in a basement, Pepper might have even enjoyed the walk.

The crowd thinned by the meter as she made her way back in the direction in which she'd come, until Pepper found herself the only soul in the street. She let herself wonder for a moment if maybe this was just normal for a Wednesday night in Dublin.

But nothing about this day had been normal.

She decided it was best not to ask herself too many questions. She'd just drive herself crazy with not knowing the answers. Any oddity that gnawed too hard, that stuck with her until this thing was over—those she'd ask the General when it was all done.

Beginning with what all this had to do with a dragon.

She'd cross that bridge when she came to it. At present, she had an actual, physical bridge to cross.

A fog had begun to gather on the river. It covered the deck of the bridge, swirling at Pepper's feet and making the bridge's white rails and arches seem suspended over nothing. The fog absorbed the lamplight just enough to cast everything in a dim golden glow.

The fog grew thicker as Pepper made her way across the bridge; it had become as thick as pea soup by the time she stepped off the other side. In every direction, all she could see was golden, glowing fog. The Labyrinth had gone eerily dormant and for the first time Pepper realized how much she'd begun to rely on its temperature shifts to tell her whether she was headed in the right direction.

For the moment, she had no direction at all. General McCaslin had only given her directions to the other side of the bridge. On the one hand, she wasn't in any real hurry to get on with things and head into Nazi Germany, but on the other hand she had never been good at patiently waiting for anything. She could only hope she wouldn't be standing out in the fog for too long.

A car started just to her right, and Pepper jumped at the unexpected noise. The running engine was nearby; had the fog not been so thick, she'd surely have seen the thing and not been so startled by it. She felt silly for a moment; she'd known a car would be coming for her. But she let that feeling pass as quickly as it had come on. It wasn't at all abnormal for a person to be startled by a loud noise they hadn't seen coming. And besides: no one had seen her reaction, there was nothing to be embarrassed about.

She could hear the car's engine as it drew closer. Careful not to look behind her, Pepper took a step backwards—toward the bridge and away from the street. If her visibility was this lousy, so was the driver's, and the last thing she wanted out of this day was to be the casualty of an auto accident.

She had to go and save magic. Getting run over by a car just wasn't on her agenda.

It was only a moment before she was able to make out the bonnet of a large black sedan as its headlights cut a bright white swath through the gold-hued fog on all sides of her.

The car pulled directly in front of Pepper and stopped. She took a moment to feel grateful it wasn't the car she'd been suspicious of earlier. That one had looked like every other Irish sedan of recent vintage. This one was larger, more a roadster than a sedan, with a long-ish front and a tight passenger compartment at the rear. And it had left-hand drive, marking it as not-at-all Irish, and not at all ordinary.

At least the whole thing was visible and not just the door; a minor improvement over the tavern from whence she'd just come.

She could hear the driver getting out, but through the fog

she couldn't see him. It wasn't until he came around the front of the vehicle, passing through the beams of its headlights, that she got a look at him. He was tall, broad-shouldered, and dressed in a black wool chauffer's uniform. This had to be her ride.

A pit began to form in Pepper's stomach. She swallowed her fear as she drew closer to the car. The driver was standing beside the car's open rear door—a clear gesture to Pepper that she should get inside.

She tried not to think too hard about where she might be headed as she climbed into the car and settled on the shiny blue leather seat. If the General had been telling the truth, she had more information coming before she'd be expected to engage any enemies. Wherever this car was taking her would be someplace safe.

Pepper forced herself to concentrate on that as the driver shut the car door behind her.

The moment she was fully inside, Pepper heard an engine crank someplace nearby. Headlights streamed in through the rear windshield as her driver threw himself behind the wheel and started the car forward, before he'd even gotten his door fully closed.

"What is it?" she asked, "what's going on?"

But her driver didn't answer. His attention was fixed on the road ahead—what he could see of it, anyway. He'd put the accelerator pedal down, shifting gears rapidly as the car sped up. He steered hard, changing lanes one after the other, back and forth across the dotted center line, pursued closely by a pair of headlights so bright she could easily see the bright blue of the roadster's interior.

Pepper tried her best to see out the windshield, but the fog was so thick and the driver's tactics so aggressive it made her too nervous. She looked out the back again, trying to make out the vehicle on their tail.

Was it possible it was the car she'd seen at the depot? Was it possible she'd been being followed this whole time?

She couldn't tell. But it would have made sense. Being followed by two men in a car and then aggressively pursued by them was at least a not-unreasonable series of events; they were two things that seemed perfectly sensible when placed one-after-the-other, even though the why and the wherefore as to anyone chasing her at all didn't add up in any reasonable fashion.

The car took a hard right, flinging Pepper across the slick leather seat.

"Ouch!" she cried as her shoulder slammed into the window crank's silver handle.

The driver didn't so much as acknowledge her.

Pepper supposed that was for the best. Seeing as they were being chased through the streets of a major city at dangerously high speeds through a fog so thick she could barely make out the silhouette of the pursuing vehicle, it was probably to her advantage that her driver's gaze, and his full attention, were firmly focused on the road ahead.

But that didn't make her any less irked.

Pepper scrambled back up to look out the rear windscreen. She sat up on her knees, gripping the seatback extra firmly in case of another unexpected whip around a corner.

The other car was getting closer—its headlights shifting from an amorphous blob of light in the fog behind them into two distinct beams of white.

"They're gaining on us!" she shouted forward, not expecting a response, but figuring the driver would want the information nonetheless.

She was pretty sure she felt the car speed up. She didn't know much about cars, but remembered having read somewhere that a roadster like this one had a top speed of over 100 kilometers per hour. Pepper couldn't imagine that was a safe speed on city streets, so she had to consider that whoever was chasing her must be even more dangerous than racing through Dublin to evade them.

Car horns blared out of nowhere. She heard the sound of a crash. Both were frighteningly nearby.

Pepper was suddenly thankful for the fog. Whatever calamity they had just so narrowly missed had at least been hidden from her view.

The car took a hard right, then a left, then left again. This time Pepper managed to hang on tight enough not to be tossed about the cabin.

Pepper tried not to think about how close they were to the river. One wrong turn, one missed corner... She did her best to put that out of her mind and turned her attention back out the rear windscreen.

The other car wasn't gaining on them anymore, but they weren't losing any ground, either.

She heard a foghorn sound.

Were they near the bay? It was bad enough to be careening through the city so close to the river, but adding a much larger and deeper body of water to the list of hazards was a whole new level of terrifying.

The foghorn sounded again. This time it was much closer.

Pepper turned in the direction of the sound just in time to see what she was pretty sure was the closed gate to a ferry dock. Its blinking red light and striped barrier arm were the first objects she'd been able to make out this whole time. She could also see the lights of a boat that had just departed, growing smaller and more distant just beyond the gate.

The gate was dead ahead, and they were far too close already. They were going to crash into it head on, there was no stopping that. What's more, the driver wasn't slowing down.

Pepper braced herself, turning to sit on the seat properly and wedged herself in as best she could—with her feet flat against the back of the driver's seat and grabbing hold of the velvet arm rest with both hands. She squeezed her eyes shut and waited for the inevitable impact.

But none came.

Chapter 12

"Dammit!" Cav slammed his palms into the steering wheel of the Vauxhall 10-4 before balling them into fists and repeating the gesture. Beside him to the left, his partner sat pressed firmly into his seat, his hands gripping, white-knuckled at its edges.

"Wha...?" Horton tried to say something, but his voice got caught in his throat.

Cav glanced charily at McDavish where he sat, but only for a moment. He ran his fingers through his already-tousled hair and looked back out the windshield. They were mere inches from the ferry dock's guard arm. His quick slam on the sedan's brakes had kept them from hitting it, a blessing to be sure. But still a frustrating conclusion.

He'd been pleased enough at himself for keeping up with their quarry. Had he expected a high-speed vehicle chase, he'd have probably insisted his partner do the driving; his experience with right-hand drive automobiles was limited at best. But in the end he was glad his partner hadn't been behind the wheel.

This had been no ordinary car chase.

He'd done an admirable job at keeping up, but the outcome remained that Pepper Jones had once again eluded them. And this time, Cav didn't need to look at the Compass Rose to tell him where she'd gone.

"Good God, man," Horton finally exhaled. His voice was hoarse and raspy but the force of his sentiment coming through loud and clear nonetheless. "What in bloody hell was that?"

Cav turned his head and balked. He wasn't sure he'd ever heard his partner use an oath like that. But, then again, if ever there was an occasion for swearing, this just might be it. Cav himself wasn't far from swearing; he'd been close enough the whole time he'd been chasing that roadster, and he was even closer now.

Because it was becoming quite clear he owed his partner an explanation.

Problem was: Cav wasn't sure he really had an explanation—at least not one he was sure Horton wasn't going to dismiss outright as hogwash.

Horton considered Arcanology a discipline no different than cryptography or aerodynamics. It was a subject to be studied, understood, harnessed for the good of King and Country. But it was nothing special.

He had no concept of magical energy as a living, working, present force.

Cav wasn't sure he was the right person to explain all this, or even that he had a deep enough understanding or a broad enough vocabulary to not sound like an utter fool in trying. He closed his eyes and took a deep breath before looking over at his partner.

He'd been doing his best to avoid this line of conversation since they'd first lost Pepper Jones on the sidewalk in Donegal.

"It's the..." he began—but he stopped short. He wasn't sure about much in this moment, but he was sure enough that he needed to approach this explanation *just so* to keep Horton on board with him. "It's a phenomenon called," he began again, "the Twist."

"Come again?" Horton asked. He frowned in Cavill's direction as he tentatively let loose his death grip on the leather seat.

"It's the Twist," Cav said again, more confidently this time. "It's... it's part of how this thing works."

"The talisman, you mean?"

"Yeah."

A car horn sounded behind them and Cav realized he'd accidentally come to a stop blocking a cross street. He put on the signal, pulled the still-running car into traffic along the quay, and continued.

He wondered if Horton had noticed how quickly the fog had dissipated. The night was once again as clear as it had been when they'd first pulled away from the Dublin bus depot.

"It allows her access to places we can't even tell are there," he said.

"The Twist?"

"I know it sounds weird," Cav qualified. "But it's a real thing. You saw her vanish on the sidewalk in Donegal."

"I saw no such thing," Horton contested.

"Sure you did." Cav shook looked over at Horton as he brought the sedan to a stop at a red light. "You didn't believe your eyes because what you saw was impossible, so you decided you couldn't have seen it. But you did see it."

Horton grumbled. He fidgeted in his seat as the car started moving again. But he didn't attempt to argue.

"And we've been chasing her in and out of it since we got to Dublin," Cavill added, doing his best to look over at his partner even while keeping one eye on the road. "And I'm pretty sure we followed her in a couple of times. Did you wonder how all that fog rolled in—so thick we could barely see—in the space of time it took us to drive around a block? Or why Pepper Jones crossed a footbridge and then turned right around and crossed it the other way?"

"I thought perhaps she'd taken an unintended turn," Horton replied.

"Nah, man," Cav shook his head. He turned the car away from the quay and back toward Dublin town center. "She went somewhere. Thing is—we went somewhere, too. It wasn't a coincidence the only road we could take was the one she came back to."

"This is poppycock," Horton said, but Cav could tell by his tone he only half believed his own assertion.

"You know it isn't," he countered. "Just like you know that roadster disappeared from sight, same as Pepper Jones did, and just like you know as soon as we weren't chasing it anymore, the fog was gone like it was never there."

"The Twist?" Horton asked, working the sound over in his mouth like he was trying to figure out what it tasted like.

"Yeah. It's really somethin'. And it's part of why we want this thing. I can scarcely begin to imagine what use power like that could be to the Allies."

"I must say I cannot imagine it at all."

"Yeah, all right," Cav said with a chuckle. It was somewhere between bothersome and comical how quickly Horton had returned to his normal self.

"But if I do allow myself such a feat of imagination," McDavish posited as the car sped down a main city thoroughfare, "and we do suppose that your Miss Jones has, for the time being, disappeared into the Twist, what should we be doing next?"

"You know, I have no idea." Cav shrugged.

Horton scowled.

"But," Cav added, "I know who will."

"You do?" Horton asked as Cav followed a sign taking them to the N4 motorway.

"Get comfy there, McDavish," he said, "we're going to talk to Flower."

Chapter 13

Pepper wasn't sure how long she'd sat there—braced for impact with her eyes closed and her breath held—but she knew it had been longer than it ought to have taken for the car to crash.

She had no idea what was happening, but it felt peculiarly like... nothing at all.

Was she dead? Was this what death felt like?

Pepper exhaled sharply and decided that couldn't be it.

She unclenched her jaw, then slowly allowed her eyes to open as she lessened her white-knuckled grip on the road-ster's arm rest. When none of those things appeared to have spelled calamity, Pepper uncurled her body, placing her feet back onto the floorboard and sitting up straight enough to once again be able to see out the window.

Except there was nothing to see.

The fog of the city had been replaced by a darkness so complete Pepper wasn't sure she'd ever seen anything like it. There was no moon in the sky that she could make out, no visible stars. She turned her gaze forward; even the roadster's headlamps were out.

They hadn't crashed, so that was something. Just what that was remained to be seen, but Pepper couldn't help but notice her driver's bearing had changed. He was no longer sitting up straight, his leather gloves straining at the intensity of his grip on the wheel. He looked almost relaxed now—comfortably seated with his head against the headrest and his hands comfortably holding the wheel steady.

She had to take it on faith that meant they had managed to lose their pursuers.

The darkness was complete, consuming and unsettling. But it was better than the fog and the panic.

Pepper lost track of time pretty quickly as she and her driver traveled through the darkness. Not that it mattered how much time was passing—she had no idea where she was going nor what the travel time was supposed to be. Patience had never been her most prominent virtue, but in this case she had little choice but to exercise it.

More than once, she'd opened her mouth to inquire of her driver—perhaps he'd be open to conversing now that the immediate danger seemed to have passed—but the words never came. After a while she'd settled into the silence, letting her body recover from the adrenaline of the high-speed chase.

Occasionally she'd turned her attention back out the window, straining her eyes for some hint of building or of countryside. But there was nothing. Nary a streetlight nor a passing car nor any dwelling in the distance broke up the all-consuming blackness.

At some point during one of Pepper's moments of distraction, a stillness had settled over the journey; a feeling that was at the same time somehow comforting and eerie as hell. Sometime in the interminable darkness, she'd stopped hearing the rumbling of the engine, stopped feeling the texture of the road, stopped feeling the tiny drafts of air sneaking in through the seam between the front and rear windows.

Pepper wasn't sure she'd ever been so still in her whole life. And having this experience while within a moving car was nothing short of bizarre.

She turned to the Labyrinth for guidance—holding her wrist out in front of her and making the charm dance as it dangled. Pinching it, pressing it to her forehead, straining to make out its lines in the pitch darkness; she tried everything she could think of to get it to react. But it did not. The Labyrinth hung there like any mundane piece of jewelry. Not that she'd expected more. Pepper knew she had negligible magical power of her own and, as such, there was little chance she'd ever be able to use the Labyrinth to its full potential.

But the thing had been plenty awake a few times already

during this quest and she was sure trying to get in tune with it wouldn't be such a bad use of her time. If she could find a way to use it—even a little—or to understand it better, then she figured she might be a good bit more prepared for whatever was ahead.

In Nazi Germany and otherwise.

At some point in the midst of her fruitless attempts to make the Labyrinth respond, Pepper became aware of a change in momentum—a slowing of the vehicle in which she was riding. How it was possible to slow down from a condition of absolute stillness baffled her to no end, but that was undoubtedly the experience of the moment.

She became aware again of the sound of tires on gravel, and the almost inaudible squeal of brakes as the driver shifted into a lower gear. The car slowed further as it rounded a corner, the first in what might have been hours of travel, but even at low speed Pepper wasn't sure how the driver was able to navigate.

It was still pitch dark. And he hadn't so much as switched on the roadster's headlamps.

The clouds parted then, giving way to a sliver of moonlight. Pepper turned toward the window, straining her eyes for anything that might give her some indication of where she was.

What little she could make out gave her pause. This didn't look like any part of Ireland she'd ever heard of.

Buildings on both sides of the street had been reduced to rubble, crumbling facades, and collapsed roofs; pockmarked walls and empty doorways made up the entirety of what she was able to make out. There wasn't a single building she could see that seemed unscathed.

"Where...?" she began to ask her driver as the car slowed further, "where are we?"

He didn't answer, instead he stopped the car, pulling over to the side and cutting the engine.

"Where are we?" Pepper asked again. But she was too late—the driver had already opened the door and stepped out of the vehicle. Before she had the chance to ponder whether she was supposed to get out as well, the curb side door came open. The driver stood with one hand on the car and the other gesturing toward an awning just across the cobblestone sidewalk.

Had this been any ordinary circumstance, Pepper would hardly have found the awning at all noteworthy. It was the long and narrow kind, signaling a walkway from just beyond the street to a door in the adjacent building. Crimson red, and with gold fringe on all sides that matched the color of the brass poles holding up the thing, it reminded Pepper of a trip she'd once taken with her father to one of Seattle's finer dining establishments. The door at the far end reminded her similarly of such a place—all brass and glass and manned by a burly-looking maître'd.

The odd thing about this awning was how it appeared to be the only whole and unsullied thing around. As far as Pepper could see, up and down both sides of the street, the area had been reduced almost entirely to rubble. Stranger still was the fact the building beyond the door appeared to be in similar trim—little more than a pile of scree.

Why then was there a pristine red awning leading to a gorgeous door in the building's façade?

Pepper was pretty sure she was about to find out. Her driver was gesturing toward the building, and she watched as the maître'd took hold of the door handle. This was apparently the destination. With a shrug and a sigh, Pepper stepped from the car.

She'd come this far. And a pretty door in a bombed out building was hardly any more bizarre than an address that may not have existed, a stairwell inside a fireplace, or a note inside of a fish. This was just one more in a series of strange doors that had begun to punctuate this adventure.

So when the maître'd pulled it open and gestured for her to enter, Pepper Jones did so without hesitation.

Chapter 14

The scene on the other side of that door was perhaps the last thing Pepper Jones might have guessed she was about to come upon. But, then again, nothing since the bus from Ardara had been exactly-as-expected. She paused in the doorway to take in the lay of the place.

It was dark inside. But not blacked out city dark like outside—more like seedy nightclub dark. The walls were draped with jewel-tone silks, and the little lamps that burned on the tables gave off hardly enough light for the people sitting at them to see one another.

A cigarette girl was wandering the crowd, her tray at just the right height to miss the tops of the glasses that seemed to be on every table. Couples huddled in upholstered booths around the back, and peals of unnaturally loud laughter erupted at intervals from all sides. Someone slid a glass of champagne into Pepper's hand, but she'd been looking the other way when it happened, so she had no idea who it had been nor where they had gone afterward.

All her attention in that moment was directed at the stage.

Situated at the far end of the room, the elevated stage was lit from behind with intense magenta light. A ten-piece band was onstage playing soft, upbeat jazz. They looked almost unreal—just a bunch of shadows against the backlit cyclo-rama, but they played well. It was nice to see light and hear music after the interminable journey through silence and darkness that had brought her here.

A woman in a scandalous costume that would not have been out of place in even the seediest of traveling circuses approached Pepper and waved her hand.

"*Komm*," the woman said. Come.

Pepper figured she ought to do as she was told. She let the woman lead her through the tangle of wire-frame chairs and café tables toward the stage. Pepper was careful not to spill champagne on anyone as they weaved and zagged their way through the crowd of revelers.

They were all the way to the front of the room when the woman finally stopped. She gestured to a table just at the apron of the stage, with a single chair behind it and a tele-phone sitting on top. Pepper had noticed similar phones on several of the tabletops as she'd passed, but had absolutely no idea what business such a thing had on the table of a nightclub.

Not that she was about to ask.

Pepper took the seat she was offered, soliciting a nod from her guide before the strange woman walked away. Setting down her bag and glass, Pepper moved to take off her hat.

She looked down at the champagne fizzing in its coupe. It was a little bit mesmerizing, watching the bubbles move through the liquid almost to the tune of the music as it drifted through the magenta light off the stage. A drink didn't sound too bad at the moment, but Pepper wasn't sure whether the General's prohibition against accepting hospitality extended this far. And she also figured she'd be needing her wits about her. One drink might just be enough to calm her nerves into submission, but it also could be too much. Seeing as she was quite sure this place was laced with magic, maybe she should let the champagne alone.

Pepper folded her hands on the tabletop beside her hat and wondered what she was supposed to do next.

For a moment she considered calling over the cigarette vendor. She'd never been much of a fan of smoking, but in this place it seemed the thing to do. Smoke hung about this room in rings and bands, swirling from the ends of cigarette holders and tobacco pipes up into the air and toward the stage in patterns that almost looked intentional.

Pepper was beginning to have a very strong feeling she

wasn't in Ireland anymore.

At least this didn't seem like Ireland. In fact, nothing about this place felt like Ireland. She'd resided on the Emerald Isle for going on two years and she had never so much as heard of anyplace at all like this one.

How long had she been in that car?

Because she had a pretty good guess as to where she was right now. It felt impossible, but so had a lot of things lately. And if she was where she guessed she was—if she was where the General had said she was going—then she hadn't any of the local currency. Trying to negotiate an exchange with the cigarette girl would probably be more trouble than it was worth.

The stage lights went out then, causing Pepper to sit up straight in her seat. Was this a cue for something?

It was only another moment before she understood. It was a cue, just not for her.

The cyclorama lit up again in an instant, bright white this time, and lights from both sides of the stage came up on the band as they began to play much louder than before.

"*Meine Damen und Herren*," a disembodied voice called over the loudspeaker. "*Bitte heißen Sie herzlich willkommen: Fräulein Holde Berge!*"

"Yep," Pepper whispered under her breath, "definitely not Ireland."

As the audience burst into applause, a performer stepped

onto the stage. She was a tall woman with henna-red hair, wearing too much rouge and a turquoise sequin gown with feather trim. Pepper couldn't decide whether Fräulein Holde Berge was wonderfully exquisite or terribly tacky. But, then again, that's how she was finding much of this place.

A spotlight struck in the back of the room, finding the performer as she stepped to center stage. Its bright light glinted off the silver microphone in her hand as she brought it to her mouth and began to sing.

Pepper thought she recognized the tune, but the German lyrics were unfamiliar enough she couldn't be sure. The singer was good, though, and for that Pepper was grateful. If she was going to have to sit around a smoky nightclub in some unknown location whilst having absolutely no idea what she was supposed to do next, at least she was being pleasantly entertained.

As Holde Berge started in on the song's second chorus, the phone on Pepper's table rang. She jumped in her seat, then scrambled to pick it up, pulling the receiver off the cradle in a mad rush to keep it from ringing a second time. But she hesitated before putting the receiver to her ear. What was the etiquette in this place? Was it rude to answer the phone while a performer was on stage? Should she have just let it ring? Should she hang it back up?

Pepper was looking around, unsure. Were any of the other patrons using the telephones? She was scanning the crowd for some idea when the singer caught her gaze from the stage. She grinned at Pepper and nodded, as she subtly gestured to the phone on the table.

Pepper nodded back and put the receiver to her ear.

"Hello?" she said softly, doing her best to cover the mouthpiece with her hand so as not to disturb the patrons around her.

"Come with me," the voice in the telephone said.

Pepper frowned. What the hell was that supposed to mean?

She looked up, confused. Who was she supposed to go with? Pepper scanned the room again, less frantically this time, trying to identify just who might be on the other end of the line.

When she glanced back at the stage, Pepper realized Holde Berge was still looking down at her. Suddenly, things clicked into place. She hung the phone gently back on its cradle and nodded back up at the woman on the stage.

The singer turned then, away from the crowd, stepping upstage and gesturing for Pepper to follow. She stepped out of the spotlight—but at the same time appeared to still be standing there. Had it not been for several things she'd already witnessed during this adventure Pepper might have found the whole thing unbelievable. But she'd learned to believe her own eyes, and she knew what she was seeing.

This woman had somehow split herself in two... or created

a double of herself... or was casting an illusion that could hold a microphone.

Or maybe the version of herself walking offstage was the illusion. Pepper wasn't quite sure, and she had neither the time nor the brain power to try and puzzle it out. She was content with the notion that it probably didn't matter. What she was sure about, the thing that did matter, was that she was supposed to be following the singer as she left the stage.

Pepper snatched up her hat and bag and crept along the apron of the stage, trying her best not to block anyone's view of the show as she went. As she reached the proscenium, Pepper was both relieved and befuddled by the fact it seemed no one had noticed what was happening. The crowd appeared fully enraptured by the singer as she started into the song's final verse. They were either unaware the woman on the stage had just split herself in two, or this phenomenon was so commonplace in this venue that it no longer qualified as noteworthy.

Pepper wouldn't have bet on either one.

As the singer stepped off the stage into the wings, Pepper found the edge of the proscenium curtain and ducked behind it. She was halfway expecting someone to try and stop her, and yet she wasn't really surprised when no one did.

Chapter 15

Pepper followed the glint of sequins through the dim wings beside the stage, down a short series of uneven stairs, and into a long, narrow hallway. The light down here was greenish and sickly, the tile floor was chipped in places and caked with what might have been a century's worth of filth; it reminded her a little bit of Camp Harmony.

That couldn't be good.

Holde Berge stopped in front of an open door with a pasteboard star in peeling gold paint hanging on it by a rusty nail. She gestured Pepper inside, then followed, closing the door behind them.

"So you have come to save the world," the singer said. Her accent was thick, and decidedly German. Pepper could only hope she'd continue to speak slowly.

"I," Pepper looked for the right way to answer, "I guess I

am. The General in the basement was a little light on the details—something about stealing a rock from the Nazis."

Holde Berge laughed then. It was a genuine, deep belly laugh, and Pepper found it as odd as she had the peals of laughter in the nightclub. Seeing as the world was at war, the very building they were standing in was barely standing at all, and she'd just been told she was going to have to save the world, Pepper Jones could find very little reason for laughter.

Perhaps, neither could Holde Berge.

Her laughter lasted barely a moment before devolving into what sounded more like a sob, then a sniffle.

The singer shook her head as she sunk onto a threadbare velvet settee in the corner of her dressing room. It rocked on uneven legs as she settled in. Pepper's guess was that the thing had once been red, its current dingy pink an effect of age and misuse.

The whole dressing room seemed to be a master class in neglect. The dressing table itself was painted either white or beige—Pepper couldn't tell beneath the layers of old caked makeup and general filth that coated it. The green vinyl of the wire-framed stool behind it was spilt in two places, and the mirror above it was chipped at the corner and cracked near the bottom along nearly its entire width. A shelf by the door housed wigs in various stages of being styled, all on wig heads missing some bit of their face or another. A costume rack along the wall was sagging under the weight of gowns and boas, all of them shedding sequins or feathers, many with ragged hems or torn sleeves.

"The General knows what she knows," the singer replied. "She has her own reasons for wanting you to succeed. But there is truth she would not have shared. There is truth of such little consequence to her she would not have bothered to share. But that truth is of great consequence to the rest of us. And that is what I know; now you will know what I know. Please, sit."

Pepper looked around and tried to discern exactly where she was supposed to sit down. She decided on the stool by the vanity, pulling it out from under the grimy table and perching herself on it facing her hostess.

"So…" Pepper said, "saving the world; things of great consequence?" She realized once she'd said them her words likely made it sound like she was completely flip about what was going on. She had a bad habit of that—of sounding as though she was making light of a situation when really the trouble was she hadn't managed to quite digest just how heavy things actually were.

Fortunately, Holde Berge seemed to take no offense. She sat forward then, causing the settee to tip again, and steadied both her seat and herself by bracing her elbows on her knees.

"Do you know of the *Thule Gesellschaft*?" she asked. Her lower lip was trembling, but her voice was smooth and calm.

Pepper shook her head. "The Thule Society?" Pepper shook her head again, although she was grateful for the English translation.

"Only what the General told me."

"And what did she tell you?"

Pepper strained to remember. What had the General said about the Thule Society? Her brain had pretty much stopped listening after the words "save magic" and "Nazi Germany" and she realized now that she probably should have paid better attention.

"They're a cult, right?" she asked. "And they're trying to control magic?"

Holde Berge nodded her head again.

"They are a cult," she confirmed, her voice suddenly strident as a vein in her forehead pulsed prominently. "They are a cult of the worst sort of people. They have power. More power than anyone figured they could possibly have and they are about to try and use that power to stop anyone who isn't a member of their cult from being able to access magic."

"Right," Pepper said. "And because of this mystical stone thing I'm supposed to be going after, there's a chance they could do that."

"More than a chance," the singer replied. "They can do it and they will do it." She brought her hands up to cover her face as she shook her head again. "I warned them," she said then, standing up and placing her hands against her thighs as she sucked in a slow, deep breath. "I tried to. I knew they had the power—I said they had the power. We should never have let that stone fall into the hands of these Nazis!" Berge tugged absently at her wig and then shrugged in Pepper's direction. "But no one listened to me," she said. "No one believed these people capable of the thing they are so determined to do."

"How come?" Pepper asked.

"How come?"

"Yeah. How come nobody believed you? How come nobody thought they had the power?"

"Because they shouldn't," Berge replied. "They started out as hobbyists, believers in mysticism, but none of them users of arcane energy—not at the beginning. But their recruiting has been in the service of giving themselves arcane power, and so now they possess a great deal. I have been monitoring their rise since they first re-formed. They were a concern, but an unlikely threat. Until Herr Himmler, that is."

A shudder went down Pepper's spine. Himmler was a name she knew. Commandant of the Nazi SS, he was a known occultist, a fervent anti-Semite, and the architect of a great deal of terror across Europe. If what was going on here had anything to do with Heinrich Himmler, it was a much bigger deal than the General had let on.

Pepper might have preferred being sent to slay a dragon.

"Himmler is involved?" Pepper asked.

"He is," Berge replied. There were visible tears in her eyes. "Who'd have thought a chicken farmer from Bavaria would grow to be such a thorn in our sides?" she let out a soft chuckle as a tear fell from her left eye onto her cheek. "There is something called the Vril," she went on. She stood up a little straighter and face was suddenly all business. "It is a kind of arcane energy—powerful, although not well understood. Himmler and his kind think it can be put into the service of only those with pure, Aryan blood."

"Gross," Pepper said. She hadn't so much meant to say that out loud, but it was how she'd felt about all the racial programming she'd been exposed to since the start of this war. It made her think of Camp Harmony and all the people her own government was trying to steal power from.

And that made her angry.

It seemed as though her one-word commentary hadn't made her hostess angry, though. And that was good. Pepper had a bit of a habit of letting her mouth pop off in ways that sometimes got her into trouble. She was glad this wasn't going to be one of those times.

"Himmler is an ass and a buffoon," the singer said. "But he is powerful, and the magic they call Vril is powerful. And the cult at Wewelsburg grows more powerful every day."

"That sounds ominous."

"Indeed it is. And the stone," she continued, "this thing we should have never allowed to come into their possession—it is perhaps the most powerful magical item currently known to exist. It absolutely could allow them to do as they wish—to focus the entire world's arcane energy so that the Twist can be accessed only by those with their particular attenuation."

"And that's really possible?" Pepper asked. It seemed like too much. It seemed like the kind of evil plot someone would write into a dime novel, not like the kind of thing that could really be done. All the world's magic just seemed too big to corral.

"With this item, and the power of the cult of the Vril, it absolutely is." Holde Berge's hands were shaking. For a moment, all of her was shaking.

"It should never have come to this," she snapped. "There are powerful people—powerful beings—they were not concerned about allowing the gem into Nazi hands. They thought it would be safe. They thought there was no way. I tried to warn them. I told them these people... They are so evil and so.... But no one listened. No one believed me and now we are here. I knew they would find a way and now they have found a way and I knew. I knew! And everything is at stake now—the whole world and all of magic, and all of us. If they do this thing—and they are going to do this thing..."

"And I'm supposed to stop them?" Pepper interrupted.

It might have been rude of her, but her hostess had clearly gone quite off the deep end. She was ranting. Pacing and wailing, with tears falling freely and feathers flying from her boa as she gesticulated. And sitting here listening to an un-hinged cabaret performer go off about warnings not heeded wasn't getting her any closer to understanding what she was being asked to do.

Holde Berge froze in place at the question. She was stand-ing with her back to Pepper; her chin fell to her chest and her hands to her sides.

"*Ja*," she answered in German with a word that Pepper un-derstood. She turned then, brushing tears from her cheeks with the palm of her hand as she did. She took a step toward Pepper and ducked a little to examine her reflection in the vanity mirror. "That is why you are here," she said then, still looking past Pepper and into the mirror as she blotted away smeared mascara from her face. "You understand, don't you—that if they succeed, the war is lost? That, indeed, all is lost if they manage to bring this plan to fruition?"

"I think so." Pepper nodded. The truth was, she did un-derstand. She just didn't want to think about it. She didn't want to think about Nazi magic being the only magic on the planet. She couldn't imagine a future where that was the case. She was afraid if she allowed herself the thought, she might come just as unhinged as Holde Berge had just been.

And that would be helpful to absolutely no one.

"The ritual is planned for moonrise," Holde informed her, the singer's voice once again sounding measured and pleas-ant—with no hint at all of the desperation and rage she'd exhibited just a moment ago, "two days from now. You must go to Wewelsburg Castle and disrupt it. We have done all we can do to help, including seeing to it that Herr Himmler will not be present to perform the ritual himself."

"And you think they'll go ahead without him?"

"There are conditions required," the singer said, "celestial conditions. If the ritual cannot be performed in two days then it will be months before they are able to make another attempt. And the war is going poorly for Germany now; they cannot risk the wait. Von Sebottendorf is a powerful man, nearly as powerful as Himmler himself. He's been a leader in the Thule Gesellschaft since nearly the beginning. I have no doubt in his ability to successfully complete the rite."

"Except that I'm gonna stop him," Pepper declared, standing up to look her hostess in the eye.

A magical item.

A focus.

For the first time Pepper had an inkling of why, of all the beings on this planet, she had been the one tapped for this mission. She wasn't sure how come it hadn't occurred to her when the General had first brought up the gem back in Dublin. Magical items were her father's stock and trade. They'd been a part of her life back home in Washington State same as the evergreen trees and the annual salmon catch. She knew how to spot these things, and she knew how to handle them. She even knew how to destroy them if it came to that.

And she'd be carrying magical protection; she couldn't forget about that. The Labyrinth had saved her life once, she could only hope to count on it again. Although just how powerful it was remained to be seen. Would it be enough to take on a castle full of Nazis with an item like the one she was being sent after?

"Hearing you talk about it," Pepper said, "I can see why the General would want this item so badly."

The singer narrowed her eyes but didn't say anything.

"What I need to know is," Pepper said then, suddenly feeling quite sure of herself and quite convinced that she could, in fact, save the world under these circumstances, "if I'm not able to steal this stone, how much trouble am I in if I destroy it instead?"

Holde Berge nodded her head and crossed her arms over her chest. Her adam's apple bobbed prominently in her throat as she considered Pepper's question.

"The stone is singularly powerful," she replied. "When it formed, a bit of the earth's own magic was captured within it. The General has a history with its magic, so there are personal motivations at play as well. If there is anyplace an item with that much power might be safe, it would be in the care of the Righ or one of her kind. But do not trouble yourself with its safety. Whatever McCaslin may have told you: if the item is destroyed, all is also well. What matters truly is that the Nazis are denied the chance to use the stone. We must keep this magic from Herr Himmler. Pleasing the Righ is of no real consequence compared to that."

Pepper didn't know what the singer meant by 'the Ree' or 'her kind', and she didn't honestly care to ask. Those were questions just as well answered after she'd gotten hold of this gem.

She had a fire in her belly now, the kind she hadn't felt since she'd helped break Mr. Miyamoto out of Camp Harmony. She was going to save the world, dammit.

"How do I get to this castle?" she asked.

Holde Berge turned away, opening the door and stepping back into the hallway with a flourish and a gesture for Pepper to follow. The singer reached into the bodice of her dress and withdrew a slip of paper, holding it out to her side. Pepper caught up just in time to take it from her.

"This is your ticket to Anderswo," she said, never breaking her stride. "You can reach the Bahnhof via subway. When you leave the cabaret, you turn right. Follow the sidewalk to the next major intersection. The station at Senefelderplatz will be in front of you and to the right. Take the train southbound to the end of the line. And Pepper," she added, stopping just short of the stage's side-curtains. She turned sharply, looking Pepper in the eye with an intensity that made her more than a little bit uncomfortable. "I must warn you," she said then, her voice suddenly very deep and very ominous, "magic is not free within the borders of Großdeutschland. An entire arm of the Geheime Staatspolizei is devoted to monitoring magic; those with powers have been disappearing since before the war. Using magic, even admitting you have the potential, is a grave risk."

"Grave risk," Pepper repeated, "got it." She frowned at herself. There she went again, seemingly making light of what actually sounded pretty horrible.

"Proceed with caution, Pepper Jones," the singer said, tears visible in her eyes once again, "if you wind up in Birkenau it will be the end of us all."

The singer swept past Pepper then, tossing aside the curtain before disappearing behind it, back onto the stage—leaving Pepper's brain swirling. She had no idea what Birkenau was, but it sounded bad.

And she also realized she'd never given the singer her name.

Shaking off her slightly-spooked feeling, Pepper stepped back through the side curtain and onto the floor of the cabaret just in time to see the iteration of Holde Berge she'd been talking to rejoin the one who was still onstage. Now in one piece, she continued on with a song—yet another tune Pepper thought she recognized but with German lyrics she couldn't quite place.

The audience went on watching as though nothing peculiar had happened at all. Pepper found it creepy, and she was more than glad to make her way out of the room and back onto the street.

Or at least she was until she found herself outside.

She'd forgotten in the time she'd been in the cabaret just how dark and deserted the streets were in this place.

Pepper slid her jacket over her shoulders and tucked the Labyrinth carefully inside the sleeve, once again wishing she knew more about the thing and about how it functioned. The words "Geheime Staatspolizei" and "grave risk" kept echoing in her head. She may not know the Thule Society from the Junior League, but she knew enough about the Gestapo to know she would rather not run afoul of them. And if they were after all magic, it would be awfully useful to know how to keep the Labyrinth still and silent.

She supposed Holde Berge would have warned her if the Labyrinth was going to be a liability—a beacon of magical energy summoning the Nazis to her position or some such. But there was no way to know for sure. Truly there was no way to know for sure what, if anything, the singer knew about the Labyrinth at all. Pepper herself still had so many questions about it—about its power, its limits, and its use.

She figured she'd find a lot of those answers on this quest to stop the Nazis.

But first, she had to find the subway.

Chapter 16

'Out to the right until you reach an intersection' had sounded like an easy enough instruction to follow, but with a thick cloud cover, no streetlights, no cars on the road, and no light from buildings, Pepper had to take extra care not to trip on the uneven marble stones of the sidewalk.

Even moving with such extreme caution, it wasn't long before Pepper spotted the entrance to the station at Senefelderplatz. The lights were on in the underground, giving the tile staircase and elevated green-and-white sign an oddly inviting glow.

Pepper wasn't sure how she felt about rushing into an eerily glowing, confined underground space, but she did know she had no interest at all in staying above ground in the equally eerie pitch black stillness of the deserted streets.

It was a curious relief when she reached the bottom of

the stairs and found herself standing on a subway platform populated seemingly by nothing more than ordinary folks going about their evening. There had been nary a soul on the street, but in the station there were more than a dozen people milling about, waiting for trains on both sides of the platform.

A train pulled in just as she arrived, and she realized that she'd been given incomplete information. She was supposed to be heading south, that she knew. But the trains weren't labeled eastbound and westbound; they were labeled with the name of the station where the line was to terminate.

Which way was South?

There was a map in the center of the platform. "U-Bahn BERLIN" it read in block letters in the top right-hand corner. So that's where she was. That would certainly explain the bombed-out and blacked-out streets above. Pepper wasn't sure how she felt about the fact she was already in the German capital, and she decided not to think too hard about it.

A siren sounded then. It was maybe the loudest thing Pepper had ever heard. There was instantly a low-level panic all around. Mothers held children a little closer, people scurried into the center of the station, away from the stairs. An elderly couple on a bench looked up at the ceiling in terrified anticipation.

Air Raid.

The whole station shook as the first of the shells hit.

Pepper was terrified. She wasn't going to get to any castle to stop any ritual if she wound up dead in the rubble of a Berlin subway station.

Although clearly rattled, the people around her seemed less alarmed than Pepper thought they ought to be, and Pepper couldn't understand how come. She'd seen the condition of this part of town. She knew what kind of destruction was currently raining from above. Surely those who lived here— who'd survived the shelling that had caused this condition to begin with—surely those people should be more concerned than they appeared.

But, then again, these people had survived all that and they were still here. So maybe they knew something she didn't. Maybe she was perfectly safe in this subway.

Or, rather, as safe as someone in her position could possibly be.

Another train pulled into the station, it was noticeably closer to full than the previous one, and headed in the opposite direction. When the doors opened, everyone with her in the station moved to get on.

"Is this train headed north or south?" Pepper asked to no one and everyone all at once.

Nobody answered.

"I need to go south," she said then, panic rising in her gut as the shelling got louder and the explosions closer together. She looked back at the map, trying to reconcile any station southward with the sign hung over the tracks, but the calligraphy was hard enough to read before the shelling had started; now, in the chaos of the moment, she could barely make out any of the letters.

Tones sounded, signaling the train's doors were closing, and Pepper made a choice. If this train was headed the wrong way, she didn't give a damn. She'd ride it all the way north and then turn around and ride it all the way back if she had to. She didn't know a whole lot about subway systems, but if Berlin's underground was built anything like anyplace else's, heading the wrong way—even to the end of the line before turning back the other way—wouldn't cost her much more than an hour or so. And it would be well worth it to get out from under the bombs.

She squeezed herself into one of the crowded train cars, careful not to crush the still-fresh tea rose in the lapel of her jacket.

"*Süd, ja,*" a harried-looking blonde woman answered as the doors shut. She pointed in the direction the train was headed and repeated, "*Süd.*"

Süd.

South.

As the train pulled out of the station into the tunnel, the sound of its wheels overwhelmed all other sounds. Even the noise of the shelling was drowned out. But Pepper was still on edge. She hung on tight as the train barreled southward.

The subway ride felt a little surreal at times. The train called at stations as though there was nothing at all out of the ordinary happening. Of course, Pepper figured perhaps air raids were ordinary in Berlin these days. Still, she found it odd to see people coming and going as though shells weren't falling overhead. More and more people got off the train at every stop, with very few others coming aboard to take their place. It wasn't long before Pepper Jones was the sole occupant of the entire train.

She wasn't sure she liked that.

The spike of adrenaline from having found herself caught in an air raid settled into a diffuse feeling of dread in Pepper's gut, and being alone in the subway car did nothing to quiet her discomfort.

At some point, she dared to listen closely—it appeared the shelling had, at least for a moment, come to a halt.

Even when stopped at one of the many stations the train had called on, there had been no further sounds of explosions she could make out. So that was good. She would have to come out of the subway eventually, and she reckoned she was less likely to meet an untimely death when there were no bombs falling from the sky.

Untimely death was not on her itinerary.

Pepper watched out the window as the train slowly crept above ground, then pulled past an exquisite glass gate and into a massive depot. The depot was well-lit, with signs and clocks along each of the dozens of platforms stretching out in both directions from where the subway had arrived.

A chime rang, and the doors came open. Pepper could feel the whole train shut off and power down. This had to be the end of the line. She gathered her bag and stepped off the train.

She had barely cleared the doorway when the yellow subway abruptly closed its doors and departed, leaving her alone on the platform.

There was only one other train in evidence, an almost cartoonish-looking steam locomotive hooked to a hodge-podge of old-timey and modern passenger cars, freight cars, livestock transports, and what appeared to be a circus wagon atop a flatbed.

It was bizarre, even when compared to other things Pepper had seen on this journey.

Equally bizarre for a station of this size was the fact no other passengers were in evidence. Pepper pulled the ticket Holde Berge had given her from her jacket pocket. Having not taken the time to look at it earlier, she realized she had no idea where she was actually headed. Hadn't the singer mentioned a place? G-something...?

The only "G" word Pepper could recall from that conversation was "Gestapo," and that was no help.

The ticket, it turned out, was also not helpful.

It was blank save for a few peculiar shapes at the edge.

Runes, maybe. And the ink of the watermark seemed to be shifting and rippling in her hand, making it a little bit nauseating to look at. Although the people she'd met since leaving Ardara had seemed to be sincere and straightforward, somehow the rule seemed to be that inanimate objects must all be vague and confounding.

Pepper took a deep breath and shoved the ticket back into her pocket. She looked across the station in hopes one of the platform signs would give her some info. But most of them seemed to be out of service. The few signs with a placard visible simply read "departed", including the one on the platform where a train was currently parked.

The only other people in the station appeared to be working on that train. If that was the train she was supposed to catch, someone over there would recognize her ticket.

And if it wasn't, then she'd try the next train, and the next. She could only hope she wasn't there just ahead of rush hour. If the place filled with trains that came and went faster than she could investigate, then that could be a problem. Especially if the platform signs weren't going to be any help.

Standing still and trying to puzzle out things wasn't getting her anywhere. She started toward the far side of the station.

The nearest footbridge passed over several sections of track. A ramshackle thing, built from rough-hewn planks and sections of mismatched steel pipe, it looked and felt at the same time impossibly ancient and truly temporary. Pepper was pleased it didn't sway as she crossed it.

She had to go past the glass wall and out of the station altogether to find the next walkway. This one was sturdy concrete, with glass on either side, and stone gargoyles at both ends. It was cool on that walkway, the autumn breeze causing Pepper to realize just how warm it had been on the subway.

The cool air felt nice, and Pepper paused for just a moment to take a deep breath.

An act she immediately regretted.

The smell of gunpowder, fire, and hot metal was terrible and overwhelming. When she looked off in the distance, she could see parts of the city were burning. She was still in a war zone, and she would do well to keep reminding herself of that.

Pepper bent her head to her lapel, letting the smell of the rose in her buttonhole soothe her nostrils. A few deliberate breaths of tea rose, and she kept walking, careful not to inhale too deeply again.

The final elevated walkway between herself and the train was made of brick and tile, and had an arch to it just where it passed over two sets of tracks. The stairs curved just so, making sure any crowds mounting or alighting the stairs needn't move orthogonally to the flow of traffic.

Not that it mattered tonight.

Pepper was still the only apparent passenger in the cavernous terminal.

But she wasn't completely alone.

A conductor in a smart black wool uniform stood just to the rear of the locomotive. In his hand he held a gold watch which attached to his coat via a long chain. He seemed to be studying it intently. Pepper wasn't sure how she felt about disturbing him.

She also wasn't sure how she felt about the train itself.

It was an old thing—a steam locomotive with a stack so tall Pepper understood why it had to be pulled into this platform; it wouldn't have fit beneath any of the station's many elevated walkways. There was a fully-loaded coal car behind the locomotive, followed by a pair of modern-looking passenger coaches.

Behind that sat the antique coaches and the other oddities, and behind those sat a string of cattle cars stretching past the glass wall and around the bend outside the station. Pepper couldn't see the end of the train, there were too many cars and the night was too dark.

A throng of Chinese men, looking like they'd stepped straight out of a textbook on the gold rush, were working between several of the sets of cars—shouting at each other in what Pepper was pretty sure she recognized as Cantonese. Her experience with foreign languages was limited, but her family had frequented a Cantonese restaurant when she was a child, and she thought she recognized phrases she'd once heard hollered between folks in the restaurant's kitchen.

She was still trying to suss out what all was happening, when the Conductor looked up and smiled at her.

"We've had a bit of a change in our schedule," he said to her in perfect, seemingly unaffected English. Pepper didn't know what that meant, but she knew it seemed bizarre to hear someone speaking with no intelligible accent. "I suppose you'll be needing a ride in the meantime," he said then.

Pepper nodded. She reached into her pocket and withdrew the ticket she'd been given back at the cabaret. The Conductor shook his head as he put his watch back in the pocket of his coat.

"We only punch those inbound," he said, as though Pepper had some idea what he meant by that. "Go ahead and get aboard. Take any seat you like. You'll be our only passenger on the outbound trip. The coach is all yours." He gestured to the passenger cars as he turned toward the locomotive.

Pepper nodded as she turned to go. Before she was able to take a step, the sound of an incoming train startled and overwhelmed her. What little experience she had with trains was that the noise started out as a low rumble and grew louder and more intense as the train approached. Not so this train. Seemingly out of nowhere a locomotive pulled into the station on the track just beside the one that had brought her here.

The mechanical platform sign switched all on its own, from reading nothing at all to reading "departed," the same as several others.

She didn't quite understand why a sign should read "departed" on a platform where a train had just arrived but she didn't have much time to contemplate it. She watched as the passengers began to debark. Men, women, and children, some in their night dresses, all covered in dust and soot and looking confused and terrified, piling out of packed cars that resembled closely the subway Pepper had taken to get here.

She was only allowed a moment's study of these new arrivals before the Conductor approached from behind and took her by the elbow.

"Quickly now," he said, "we must be going. If we dare to tarry, we may be pressed into service for another destination. And we wouldn't want that, now would we? If I were to take you to where they're going," he added, inclining his head toward where passengers were continuing to exit the newly-arrived train, "then I'd have to punch your ticket, and you'd not be able to get to where you're trying to go. Best be off now. You've got places to be."

He turned then, and left, walking intently toward the locomotive and hopping aboard as soon as he was in range.

Pepper was confused. This was quite unlike any train she'd ever seen, and certainly didn't resemble any railroad timetable she'd heard of. And she certainly had no understanding of how taking on other passengers might affect the validity of her ticket or the train's final destination.

But, then again, much of what she was up to was nothing like anything in her experience. And if getting on this train, at this moment, and all by herself, was the thing she was supposed to do in order to get to where she needed to get to stop the Nazis from gaining control of all the world's magic, then she wasn't about to hold things up by asking for an explanation.

Pepper shrugged and did as she'd been told, walking the length of the locomotive, past the coal car, and up the steps into the first passenger car she came upon.

The first car was one of the more modern ones, and its interior was simple, with muted blue bench seats along the windows on both sides. Some seats were facing forward, others backward. It only took Pepper a minute to realize the seatbacks were on a hinge, and could each of them be arranged either way to suit a passenger's preference.

She made her way through the first car and into the second. Finding it identical to the other, and seeing no reason at all to walk any farther, Pepper settled into a rear-facing seat near the center of the second car.

Pepper heard the telltale hiss of steam and felt the train lurch. She watched out the window as the train pulled away from the station, unable to help noticing they were leaving the entire complement of cattle cars behind in the station.

Pepper's mind flashed to the Murphys and their milk business back in Ardara. She hoped her need to get to wherever it was this train was taking her hadn't put any small farmers or ranchers in a bad place. She'd hate to be the reason a family business lost out any revenue in wartime—even German ones.

But she couldn't let that bother her. It wasn't her choice to leave the cattle cars behind—just as it wasn't her choice to leave behind the other passengers, who'd begun the process of moving off the arrival platform and onto several others throughout the station.

It wasn't even her choice to be taking this train.

She hadn't chosen this quest. It had chosen her, for reasons she did not yet comprehend.

But she had chosen to accept it. She'd made a choice to move forward at every step. Surely she could have told the General she would absolutely not be going to Nazi Germany. She could have told the cabaret singer she had no interest in fighting a powerful cult in their castle stronghold.

She was being asked to save the world. With no meaningful magic of her own and wielding a powerful artifact she hardly understood, she was being asked to save magic for the entire planet.

She reached into the sleeve of her jacket, taking firm hold of the Labyrinth between her thumb and forefinger. And she resolved to go and do just that.

No one she'd met this far on her journey seemed to have any doubt at all as to her ability to do what was being asked of her. The one thing she did understand was that her possession of the mysterious Labyrinth had made her functionally immortal—at least having given her an uncanny ability to heal herself—and she knew in her gut she had what it would take to get this job done.

But first, she needed to sleep.

She was tired—bone tired. Although she had no idea what time it was nor how long she'd been traveling, she was aware enough of her own fatigue to know she ought to try and sleep while she had a moment. There was little chance she'd miss her stop. It was already pretty clear to her this was no ordinary train. And that, coupled with the fact she was to be its sole passenger for the duration of her voyage, gave her complete confidence she wouldn't be allowed to sleep through her intended port of departure.

She wished now it had occurred to her to try and sleep during the interminable car trip through pitch dark nothingness. It might have been a better use of her time than trying to access the Labyrinth's power. She looked at the charm on her wrist; it had been still and dormant like any mundane piece of jewelry ever since she'd arrived in Berlin, with the possible exception of a chill she'd felt while aboard the crowded subway. But she'd written that off as incidental.

The Labyrinth had gone silent and she wasn't sure why.

That was one of many answers Pepper was pretty sure she'd never have—up to and including just what had allowed her to cross the channel in an automobile. That in and of itself was an odd thing—maybe the strangest happening yet in this series of strange happenings. Add to that the fact they'd come across not only the channels, but occupied France and a good chunk of Germany in what couldn't have been more than a few hours, and Pepper was more convinced than ever that she'd spent some time outside of mundane reality.

She wasn't sure what to think of that, nor was she altogether convinced she was back in the 'real world' at the moment, but she was happy enough to have been brought this far safely.

For certain values of 'safe' anyway.

She un-pinned her hat, taking it off and setting it onto the seat across from her. She set her bag down with it, and slipped her jacket off as she lay down across the bench seat before draping the jacket over herself like a blanket.

When she'd first heard she was being asked to cross into Nazi Germany, Pepper had it in her head that getting there would be most of the battle. She'd had visions of parachutes, smuggling compartments, and trying to recall her high school French lessons.

This had been easier than that. It had been strange, incredibly so, but not yet difficult. So far, the hardest part of this whole thing had been wrapping her mind around everything she'd seen since she'd been handed that giant fish back in Ardara.

But bombed-out cabarets, Suffragette Generals in tavern basements, and out-of-place Chinamen in peculiar train stations where even the arrivals were said to have departed were hardly a problem.

Or, at least, that was what she would keep telling herself.

She was different now. Mr. Miyamoto had trusted her with the Labyrinth and with all its powers. So what if she was only now learning what it all meant and how to use it? She'd been given a mission and she was going to carry it out.

No one she'd met since she'd gotten the note from the fish's mouth had seemed to have any doubts whatsoever as to her ability to do what was being asked of her. So why should she doubt herself?

Pepper looked out the window as the train reached its full traveling clip. The countryside near Berlin wasn't all that different from outside of Dublin—or, come to think of it, from outside Seattle.

It occurred to Pepper she hadn't thought to ask how far it was between Berlin and wherever it was she was being taken on this leg of the trip. Not that it mattered. She would arrive when she arrived.

As she settled her head into the crook of her elbow, she took a close look at the labyrinth dangling from the bracelet just inches from her eye.

She concentrated on that image as she closed her eyes and drifted off.

Chapter 17

The sun shone bright through the windows of the train car as Pepper's eyes fluttered open. She yawned intensely—quite sure in her own head that she hadn't gotten nearly enough rest, but equally certain the time for sleep was over. She sat up slowly, wary of the soreness she was likely to feel from having slept all night curled up on a train bench, and was surprised when no discomfort showed itself. Clearly she still wasn't used to the Labyrinth's restorative effect on her body.

Pepper took a moment to look out the window as she stretched in her seat. The train was stopped. The sun was high in the sky, and on both sides of the tracks, tall corn stalks stood in neat rows waiting their turn for their autumn threshing.

It seemed an odd choice for a train station.

This couldn't possibly be her destination.

Could it?

Pepper shook her head and reached for her hat, pinning it as best she could to cover as much of her sleep-tousled hair as possible. The train was still; it wasn't just stopped. There were no creaks or groans, no vibrations beneath the floor or seats like she'd felt at idle in the Berlin station. If this wasn't where she was going, she had time enough to find out.

And if it was...?

If this was the place she'd been headed, then it wouldn't do anyone any good for her to wait for the train to take her someplace else.

Careful not to bruise the still-fresh tea rose in her lapel, Pepper gathered her things and went to investigate.

She was barely down the boarding stairs when she spotted the clock. Wrought iron and decrepit, with no hands upon it by which to tell time, it hung from a scrollwork bracket a meter's width from the edge of the track. Beneath it hung a sign with paint so faded Pepper had to move closer to make out the calligraphy:

Anderswo

Wasn't that the name of the place Holde Berge had said she was headed? Pepper didn't remember.

Pepper wasn't completely sure she was in the right place.

But the train was stopped, there was no sign of the conductor, and a clock with no hands standing in the middle of a corn field seemed just bizarre enough to fit in with the rest of her travels.

Pepper looked to the Labyrinth for guidance, but it offered no help. It still just dangled from her wrist like a mundane bauble, as though nothing of any consequence was happening at all.

She squinted her eyes against the brightness of the sun and looked around. Her gut told her this was the place, and her gut was seldom wrong. But what next? Where to? Taking off across a field of tall corn that stretched out as far as her eyes could see didn't seem like the best of ideas, but it also seemed like the only option for a next step.

Frustrated, Pepper walked toward the locomotive; perhaps there would be a conductor or engineer in evidence who could point her in the right direction. She was supposed to be going to a place called Wewelsburg Castle; surely the men who drove the train would know how to get there from here.

But there was no sign of anyone—neither alongside the locomotive nor in its cab.

Just ahead of the train stood a barrier arm with a blinking red light that so closely resembled the one she'd almost crashed into in Dublin it gave her eerie flashbacks. Wherever she was now, she wasn't supposed to go any farther—at least not in that direction.

But where, then, was she supposed to go?

"Hello?" she called. "*Guten Tag?*" but no one answered.

Listening carefully for any sounds of bells or steam, Pepper quickly crossed the single set of tracks to look up and down the train on the other side. Finding the far side just as deserted, Pepper stalked back onto the railroad and faced the locomotive.

"What the hell?" she yelled, half expecting it to answer; that certainly wouldn't be the strangest thing to have happened to her this week. She turned her head toward the clock, with a mind to yell at it as well.

And then she saw it.

The endless fields of corn on both sides of the train stood in tight, narrow, perfectly planted rows. But in one place, just opposite the decrepit clock, it seemed a row was missing. Either it was such a subtle difference that Pepper hadn't noticed it at first, or it was like number Twenty-A Temple Bar and maybe hadn't been there at all a minute ago.

Either way, it was a path.

It was the only path.

"Yeah, okay. Sure... great," Pepper grumbled. She scowled at the narrow passage, but set off into it nonetheless.

"She's where?!?!" Flower's voice shook the windows as

Horton and Cavill sat, closer together than they might have chosen, on the tiny deacon's bench in his front room.

"At least she isn't lost anymore," Cav offered.

Horton hadn't been able to abide his partner's driving for long after their ordeal through the streets of Dublin (and maybe also not-Dublin, a possibility that Horton had yet to come fully to terms with and absolutely did not wish to discuss further), so they'd swapped seats just a few miles out of town. Cavill had been fine with this, as it had given him the ability to watch the Compass Rose as they went.

For a while there, he kind of wished he hadn't.

The thing had lost track of her entirely.

Flower, who had done all the work to anchor the Compass Rose to their target, had been thoroughly and vocally displeased when Cavill had informed him of this development upon his and Horton's arrival in Ardara.

So he'd thought their host would be pleased at the news that tonight, it had once again shown Pepper Jones's location. That prediction had turned out to be somewhat less than accurate.

"How!?!" he bellowed, throwing his arms into the air as he paced back and forth across the tiny room's threadbare rug.

"Your guess is as good as ours, mate," Horton spoke up. "If Cavill's reading is even accurate."

Flower crossed the room and had a look at the Compass Rose where it sat, open, on his coffee table.

"Oh, it's a good reading, all right," he declared. "Your Labyrinth and my Miss Jones are somewhere in the Black Forest." He slammed his hands onto his hips as he looked up at the ceiling. "But how the hell did she get there?"

"Do you think the enemy's gotten to her?" Horton asked. He'd been on the phone for more than an hour, checking in with operations back in Bletchley Park; they wanted to be sure Pepper Jones and the potent magic she carried hadn't reached enemy territory via any sort of Allied conveyance. He'd felt sure that hadn't been the case—as he would certainly be within any chain of command that involved sending an arcane power into Germany on Britain's behalf—but he felt it worth everyone's time to double check.

Because if she wasn't in Germany on Allied business, the possibility was high she was working for the other side.

"No way," Cav replied.

"You can't be so sure," Horton countered.

"Yes I can." Cav stood up and took a step toward the window. He needed some air. "And I've got a file in my locked desk drawer back at Bletchley Park to back me up. Pepper Jones hates Nazis," he stated the facts as he knew them as plainly as he could. "She hates injustice, she hates authoritarianism, and she hates it when people are mistreated. She couldn't stand the stuff she saw in our internment camps in America—that's how this whole thing got started, in case anyone was wondering how I wound up on this case. There is absolutely no way she's working for the other side."

"If she isn't working for us, and she isn't working for the Germans, what's she doing there?"

"I don't know the answer to that," Flower replied, running his fingers through his sandy-blonde hair. "But I have to agree with Weathersby's assessment of the situation. I can't imagine she's been recruited by the enemy. There's something going on here that we don't fully understand."

"Oh, you think?" Horton snapped.

Cav started at that. He wasn't sure he'd ever heard the man use sarcasm before.

"I do think," Flower snapped back. He was clearly in no mood. "I think she's in danger and there's nothing we can do about it."

"Are we sure about that?" Cav asked.

"What do you mean?" Flower asked, anger beginning to seep further into his voice.

"I mean," Cav replied, "are we absolutely sure we can't help? Do we know for certain there are no British or American arcane assets in deep cover over there who we might call on? Is there a chance there's someone over there who works for us who we could send to bring her back?"

"I highly doubt it." Horton was the one to give an answer. "If we had people on the ground in Germany, as the head of the Arcane Desk, I'd likely know about it. And I know of no such operatives."

"And even if someone like that does exist," Flower added, "it would be too dangerous—for them and for Pepper—to try and get in contact. I think we're just going to have to trust magic on this one," he said.

"I beg your pardon?" Horton asked, bristling at Flower's assertion.

"Cavill," Flower said then, all but completely ignoring McDavish's contrariness. "You said you're pretty sure she left through the Twist?"

"From right in front of us," Cav affirmed, "yeah."

"Well, if she found her way there through the Twist, we're just going to have to trust she'll find her way back the same way. We'll need to keep an eye on the Compass Rose," he said then, "we'll want to keep tabs on where she goes, and we'll want to know about it the moment she steps into the Twist again. But the thing we need to be focusing on—the thing that's going to matter to us—is trying to figure out where she's likely to walk out the other side. Because we're going to want to get there first."

Chapter 18

Pepper had never been particularly fond of the outdoors. There were bugs, and smells, and the kinds of pollen that could leave her nose stuffed up for weeks at a time. She'd always considered herself more of an indoor gal.

Owing to that, and the fact she'd grown up in urban Seattle, Pepper hadn't spent much time on farms or with farmers. That meant she had no clue about the planting of corn, which meant she had no clue about this endless field she was feeling increasingly trapped within.

She felt like she'd been walking for hours. The air was warm enough to make sweat bead on her upper lip, but not so warm as to keep her from feeling chilly without her jacket on. And the sun didn't look to have moved one iota from its position high overhead; it seemed completely fixed in the sky.

Everything seemed fixed. Immovable. Impassible.

The stillness was eerie. It was a stillness more profound and unsettling than any she'd experienced before. It was nothing like the stillness of the Irish countryside after a storm, or of the Pacific Coast at sunrise. Even the blacked-out city of Berlin, as creepy as it had been, had maintained an undercurrent of life and motion.

Here there was nothing. Not so much as the buzzing of insects nor the rustle of the stalks in the breeze. In fact, there was no breeze. The air stood as still and stagnant as the plants and the sun. It was as if everything in this place were either dead or artificial.

And Pepper did not like it one bit.

More than once she'd looked to the Labyrinth, hoping for guidance. But the magical talisman at her wrist was as still as everything else in this place.

The path had remained narrow, barely wider than her shoulders, and the unnaturally flat and even ground had been completely free of rocks, roots, or snags. She'd seen gentle hills in the field through the train window, but hadn't yet felt even the slightest incline on her hours-long walk.

Charging ever forward, the scenery never changed. Always the same stray leaf in her path on the left, always the same pile of silk on the right—always several paces ahead, never drawing any nearer.

She tried speeding up.

She tried slowing down.

She tried walking backwards.

She tried closing her eyes.

Nothing. Not one sign of any progress, not even the tiniest indicator she'd covered any distance.

Only the sweat on her brow and the blisters forming on her heels from plodding so long across soft earth told her she'd made any effort at all.

It was like some sort of impossible agricultural treadmill.

She was beginning to wonder whether she'd taken some sort of ineffable wrong turn and, instead of heading to a Castle to fight Nazis for the future of magic, was now cursed to traverse a never-ending corn field for the rest of eternity.

She looked to the sky; had the sun moved at all? Not that she was any expert on telling time by the position of the sun, but she understood the basics. The sun had been directly overhead when she'd taken her first steps onto the narrow path, so reason held that it ought to have moved in some direction by this point.

But she couldn't be sure.

Pepper shook her head. What even was this place? She hadn't been given any preparation for an interminable corn field.

There was no way to know for sure how long she'd been walking, but Pepper knew when she was too tired to go on any farther.

"This is ridiculous," she grumbled, sinking to her knees to sit in the dirt where she'd stood. She was tired, she was uncomfortable, she was lost, and she was hungry. And despite the efforts of several hours, she'd failed to make any discernable progress.

Pepper opened her purse and spent a moment digging for any remnants of the snack she'd packed herself for the trip to Dublin from Ardara. But she'd polished that off hours ago.

Days?

How the hell long had she been at this?

And how the hell long was she expected to follow this damnable path to nowhere?

Pepper leaned back, reclining against the base of a particularly hearty cornstalk, and took stock of her situation. She was damned well convinced that spending another interminable amount of time trudging through this field wasn't going to do her any good.

So what now?

She looked down the trail ahead of her, straining her eyes for any differences her change in perspective might reveal, but there was nothing. Maybe the answer was to turn around; to head back to that orphaned clock and catch another train. How long would that even take?

Holde Berge had given her a pretty tight timeline. Backtracking would cost her a good deal of valuable time.

But still, waking up on the train had been the last time

she was sure she was in the right place. Turning back seemed the best course of action under the circumstances.

Pepper turned her head in the direction from whence she'd come.

And immediately sat up straight.

Just down the path, not more than a hundred yards away, the corn rows stopped at a split wooden fence just like the one she'd passed through at the train stop. Beyond the fence lay a dense forest. Moss-covered rocks and tangles of underbrush gave way to towering conifers. Dappled sunlight filtered through the canopy, landing neatly along a narrow footpath leading up a gentle hill.

It was impossible, of course. These woods hadn't been behind her fifty paces ago when she'd looked for the sun's position, and they hadn't been there fifty paces before that, when she would ostensibly have been standing right beside that fence in the distance.

It was faerie tale impossible.

This path appearing was no more impossible than a missive in a salmon's mouth, an address that didn't exist until she looked closely for it, an overland trip from Ireland to Germany, or a singer who could split herself in two. In fact, when Pepper stopped to consider things, things were perfectly, fittingly impossible.

She scrambled to her feet and made for the woods.

Thankfully, this way lay progress, and within a few

anxious strides, Pepper neared the edge of the planted field.

She stepped through the fence and into the forest without hesitation; she'd lost enough time already, and she was sure this was the way to go. The forest was inviting at first—the moss-covered path easily discerned and the old growth canopy providing a welcome respite from the heat of the sun. The incline was gentle and the breeze smelled sweet. Even the blisters on her feet felt better as she traveled across the springy lichen.

But it wasn't long before the forest's character changed altogether. The sun was soon invisible, with only scant light filtering through the thicket. The temperature had dropped suddenly and accordingly and Pepper, still damp with sweat from the heat and exertion in the corn field, couldn't seem to keep from shivering. She slipped her jacket back on, pausing to smell the somehow still-fresh tea rose pinned to her lapel. How that flower hadn't begun to wilt or bruise was as mysterious as everything else about this whole ordeal.

She continued forward along an increasingly thorn-snarled path as the forest around her seemed to grow darker by the minute.

Pepper had never been afraid of the dark. And, before today, she'd always found peace in the gloaming. But every step she took made these woods feel more ominous. Snaps of twigs and rustles of underbrush seemed to come from everywhere and nowhere all at once, and when she dared turn her head to try and see what had made the sounds, it took her longer and longer to find the path again.

Nightfall in a foreign thicket behind enemy lines on her way to a Nazi castle was nothing at all like nightfall anyplace else. For the first time since she'd arrived safely in Ireland years before, Pepper felt frightened—truly, deeply, over-whelmingly and to the bone terrified.

It was all but pitch dark now. The path had led into a small clearing, and there was no way to see where it picked up. Pepper wasn't sure whether she was trembling from fear or from cold as she paused to sit on a large rock at the edge of the clearing. Pausing to sit in the cornfield had been the thing that led her to the path she was on, so she figured it wouldn't hurt to rest for a moment here.

She looked down at the Labyrinth where it dangled from her wrist, unresponsive. Maybe that was for the best?

Magic is not free.

Holde Berge's words rang in her memory. Maybe the Labyrinth going dormant was to protect her from being de-tected by the forces she'd come to stop. But even if that was the case, Pepper didn't find its sudden lack of feedback at all comforting.

She was deep in a foreign wood and the sun had set. What was it she'd learned in Girl Scouts?

Trying to pick up the almost-indiscernible path in the pitch darkness was probably not going to net her anything but frustration. But staying still through the October night with nary so much as a match would put her at risk for hypothermia. And whether she were to stay put or keep going, she'd still possibly need to contend with whoever, or whatever, had been making noises in the forest just out of her sight all day.

Pepper closed her eyes and took a deep breath. There were no good choices here.

What would Mr. Miyamoto have done?

When she opened her eyes, still unsure of her way forward, Pepper noticed immediately the clearing around her had changed somehow—a dappled light in hues of purple and orange suddenly fell across the forest floor.

Pepper's mouth fell open as she cast her gaze across the clearing. The light was coming through the windows of a building that Pepper was sure hadn't been there just a moment ago.

"Well I'll be damned," she whispered to herself, "Faerie tale logic strikes again."

She stood up and shook her head, unsure if she could trust what she was seeing. The building itself was odd, almost as strange in itself as the fact of its appearance. It should have been a cottage—every line and curve of the place, from its thatched roof, to its colorful window glass, to the timbers of its fachwerk, reminded Pepper of the illustrations in a faerie tale book she'd had as a child.

But the whole thing was too large. The leaded windows, the spinning weathervane, the uneven stone steps leading to the heavy wooden door, all of it seemed on an impossible scale.

And it was glowing. The whole building was glowing.

It shone like a porcelain lamp shade with the bulb turned on inside.

As bizarre as it appeared, the glow was warm and golden, and Pepper felt herself drawn to it. She reckoned she should be more terrified by the sudden and unexpected appearance of an overlarge cottage in the middle of a woodland thicket than she had been of the perfectly normal forest—and maybe she would have been if it hadn't been for the events of the past couple of days.

Her gut was telling her this place meant safety, and those kinds of bone-level feelings had never failed her before.

Not that she had too much of a choice; it was approach this building or spend the night at the mercy of the elements and whatever wild beasts might live nearby.

She picked up her purse and scrambled across the overgrown pathway toward the door.

Chapter 19

The door to the overlarge cottage dwarfed Pepper as she stood before it. It was a sturdy thing, built of weathered, heavy timber set into a carved stone doorway overgrown with ivy. For a moment, she wasn't entirely confident of her ability to open it on her own, but when she pulled lightly on the handle, it gave way easily.

Rather than stop to wonder at the physics at work, Pepper stepped through it as quickly as possible—lest the whole place disappear again before she could get inside.

The main floor of the building seemed to be laid out as one giant room, although perhaps not as large as Pepper would have estimated it from outside. Size notwithstanding, Pepper was thankful to be inside it.

The room was warm, homey and inviting. A variety of mismatched tables were arranged all along the room's perimeter—long rectangular ones along the walls punctuated by tiny round ones beneath each of the leaded glass windows, no two of them exactly alike. Small groups of people, several of them families with children, sat around the tables, eating and drinking and talking. The pianist in the corner seemed to play his upbeat pop tunes at the perfect volume to be heard over the din of the crowd but not so loud as to inhibit the quiet conversations that were going on all around.

And it smelled divine—like roast meat and baking bread, wood fires and paraffin wax. Pepper's stomach growled in response. She was all of a sudden acutely aware that she hadn't had anything substantial to eat since the bus ride from Donegal. Of all the difficulties she'd had so far, resisting food and drink while in this place was going to be a doozy.

It had been made very clear to her in Dublin that food and drink in General McCaslin's pub was a non-starter. She wasn't altogether sure of what the precise consequences would have been had she gone against the interdiction, but the impression she had from both the General and those creepy twins who'd first greeted her was that they would have been dire.

Pepper had barely made it out of the doorway when an excited youth approached her, babbling something in German that she had no way of understanding. But she was able to get the gist. He was gesticulating excitedly back and forth between Pepper and an elaborate bar that took up most of the wall to her right. She followed his lead toward the bar and took a seat on the metal barstool farthest from the door.

A woman was working behind the bar, tending to a group of weary-looking gents at the far end from where Pepper was seated. She was a tallish woman, stocky but without any sign of plumpness. Her skin was olive, and her dark hair cascaded down her back in long waves. Her face was made up; rouged cheeks and lined eyes only adding to the beauty of her naturally chiseled face. She was lavishly bedecked in beaded silks, the colors of which all but shone in stark contrast to the earthen tones of the building, bar, and furnish. She might have been the most beautiful human Pepper had ever seen.

It was warm in here—blessedly warm. And it wasn't long before Pepper was warm enough to take off her jacket. She drummed her fingers on the bar, wondering exactly where she had found herself and what she might do next. She hoped the plan might be food, drink, and a good night's rest, but she had a pretty powerful feeling that wasn't in the cards.

She had a little money in her bag, but it wasn't in Reichsmarks—only half a dozen Irish florins and a couple of American dollars she'd never bothered to take out of her purse. Although there was every chance this establishment wouldn't take any currency she'd ever heard of. If the pub in Dublin had been any indication, this place likely traded in magic— a thing she was only just coming to understand and surely couldn't put to work for her own benefit just yet.

Pepper was so lost in her thoughts that it took her a

moment to realize the woman behind the bar had turned and was now moving in her direction. She caught Pepper's gaze and smiled as she closed the distance between them.

"*Wilkommen, Fremde*," she greeted, smiling warmly as she placed her folded hands onto the bar in front of her. "*Ich habe dich erwartet. Ich freue mich, dass du es sicher hierher geschafft hast.*"

"Riiiiight," Pepper whispered, trying her best to smile back at her hostess.

Pepper knew her smile belied her discomfort. Somehow, in all the rigamarole and urgency, somehow she'd failed to realize a trip into Germany meant she was very likely going to need to converse in German. Pepper had never heard a word of German in her life until she'd approached that bombed-out cabaret in Berlin, and she wasn't sure now just how she was supposed to deal with this suddenly very obvious, very major problem.

The woman behind the bar nodded. She gave Pepper a patient smile and held up a single finger in a gesture universally recognized as 'one moment'. The woman stepped away from Pepper and turned to face the back of the bar, where she crouched down to pull open one of the ornately-carved drawers nested in the giant oak edifice.

When she turned back around, the woman approached Pepper briskly, holding up a jeweled feather for her inspection. The proprietress set the item down on the bar and pushed it toward Pepper, before pulling back her pink silk veil to reveal a similar item pinned into her hair.

Pepper reached for the jewel, looking her hostess in the eye. The other women nodded.

"*Ja,*" she said with a nod, "*ist für dich.*" She pointed down at the jewel, then to Pepper, to the gem on her own head, and back at her guest.

Pepper took hold of the thing and turned it over in her hand. The jewel was unlike anything she'd ever seen—faceted with prisms and swirls, it changed color with every angle of the light. Purple to blue to green and back, the gem's brilliance transformed over and over again as Pepper examined it. The feathers were blue and green, with flecks of magenta that showed themselves when the breeze hit the plumes.

There was a pin on the back of it, fastened to a barrette, and Pepper was sure she was supposed to pin it into her hair similarly to how her hostess had done. She set her jacket and purse on the bar in front of her and took care to un-pin her hat and remove it while doing the least possible damage to her already-untidy hairdo.

She un-hinged the barrette and slid the jewel into her hair, fastening it into a spot she could only hope didn't look too ridiculous—gemstones and feathers were hardly a match for the rest of her apparel, but she'd learned early in her association with Mr. Miyamoto that magical necessity outweighed the needs of fashion every time.

Pepper shrugged as she smiled back at her hostess.

"There now," the woman said to her, her voice sounding in perfect English with only the barest hint of an accent, "you will be able to understand us from here on out."

Pepper nodded. She could understand. She wasn't sure why or how come, but she could understand.

"Yes," Pepper said back, reaching up to touch the gem she's pinned in her hair.

"It is the gem," the proprietress told her, pulling her veil back into place on her head. "There is magic anchored inside. As long as you are wearing it, you will be able to understand us here. And those with whom you converse will be able to understand you. My name is Vadoma," she said, "and I am the keeper of this place."

"I'm Pepper Jones," Pepper replied, "and to be honest, I'm not entirely sure where I am or how I got here."

"That all depends on what you mean by 'here'," Vadoma said back. "Here is wherever you need to be."

"Ok."

"I am where I need to be," Vadoma said, "for whomever needs to find a place, and whomever needs a place to find. And today, that person is you. And so, my travel-weary friend, what may I offer you? Would you care for a cold drink? A hot meal? A night's rest?"

Pepper sighed. She wanted all those things. She wanted them all rather badly. But the words of the General in the

Dublin basement weighed heavily on her mind. She knew better than to accept hospitality inside a magical place.

But, damn, the smells in here were incredible.

Pepper had never been great at concealing how she was feeling in a given moment—particular when matters of hunger and thirst were in play. Apparently she wore her struggle across her face plainly enough that Vadoma couldn't help but chuckle.

"You are the one who was sent by the General," she surmised.

Pepper nodded. She wasn't sure whether being recognized made her more or less comfortable with her circumstances.

"It's all right," Vadoma said. "I have been expecting you."

"You have?"

"I have. And I am pleased you're here."

"That's... that's good. I guess...."

"I trust you will find it good," Vadoma said. "We are ready for you. But before we get to business, you should eat something."

Pepper shook her head and grimaced.

Vadoma laughed again.

"The General has you well-trained," she said. "But not to worry. The rules of hospitality here are not what they are where she dwells. In my tavern, the visitors get what they deserve. So please, sit. Eat and drink your fill. I promise you invite no peril in doing so."

"Oh, good," Pepper replied. "I'm kind of starving." She wasn't entirely sure she should believe what she was being told. There was every chance this hospitality was as much a trap as the beer in Dublin had almost been and that accepting Vadoma's offer of food would somehow lead to disaster.

But it occurred to Pepper that the one thing no one had done to her in that Dublin pub was to tell her lies. They'd tried to imprison her there for all eternity, but no one had made any attempts to convince her of anything untrue. In fact, the General had been quite level with her on matters of magic and entrapment and supernatural hospitality.

As outlandish and unbelievable as this whole ordeal had been, everything she'd been told had turned out to be honest and accurate. There was no reason to suspect things were any different in this place.

She decided to trust Vadoma. She wasn't sure if the feeling had its origin in her guts or her growling stomach, but she'd done well enough going with her instinct over the course of her life that she figured she might as well trust her feelings now.

Food came out in short order. A generous plate of stewed meats with potatoes and carrots was set in front of her as well as half a loaf of fresh bread and a tankard of beer. It smelled divine and it tasted like heaven.

Pepper did her best not to wolf down the meal too greedily. But she was ravenous, more so than she'd even realized, and every spoonful felt like her whole body was being replenished.

When Pepper was nearing the bottom of the plate of stew, a door beside the bar came open, and through it stepped a peculiar and exquisite woman. She moved decisively in Pepper's direction, and Pepper couldn't help but study her a bit as she drew near.

She was tall—perhaps the tallest woman Pepper had ever seen up close—and sturdily built in every dimension. Her head was shaved; she was bald save for a day's worth of stubble. Over her left eye, she wore a patch, out from which stretched a web of pink scars. Her right leg had been amputated above the knee and in its place was a remarkable prosthetic—a brass and steel contraption more intricately carved than any piece of artwork Pepper had ever seen. She was a magnificent and imposing woman.

Pepper couldn't help but stand agog as the stranger circled her with a measuring tape.

The woman said nothing as she approached Pepper from one angle and then another, and another, taking measurements of her arms, legs, head, and torso. It felt peculiar to have her measurements taken while sitting at a bar, but she hadn't been asked to move and she absolutely did not want to do anything to annoy the woman taking the measurements.

"You needn't let your food get cold," Vadoma said when she saw Pepper frozen in place in her seat.

"I thought I should hold still," Pepper replied as the tall woman wrapped a tape around her neck.

"There is no need," Vadoma assured her.

"Ok." Pepper nodded and reached up to tear off another bite of bread. She popped it into her mouth and reached for some beer, finding her arm intercepted on its way by a quick visit from the tape measure. "What's... what's she doing, exactly?"

"We are nearly ready," Vadoma answered. Pepper had no idea what that meant. "We will finish our preparations tonight," she said. "When you have eaten your fill, please head upstairs and make yourself comfortable for the night. When you awake in the morning, all will be prepared."

Pepper nodded again, her mouth full of stew. She'd spotted the narrow timber staircase when she'd first sat down. Her feet were sore and her body was exhausted, she was sure she'd have no trouble sleeping regardless of what type of accommodations she found up those stairs.

Pepper made quick work of the rest of her dinner, wiped her mouth, and excused herself. With every delicious bite closer to satiety, the possibility of sleeping in a proper bed had grown more and more appealing. It took all she had not to run full-speed up the stairs. As she climbed toward a night's rest at a polite pace, Pepper allowed her glance to linger for a bit on the happenings around the inn.

A window on the far side of the room blew shut, the gust

of wind blowing a woman's skirt onto a stray bench nail. A man knocked over his beer trying to get to her before the skirt tore. Their child danced wildly to the happy music from the piano, oblivious to his parents' moment of difficulty.

For a moment, Pepper could almost imagine herself in a perfectly normal inn.

But only for a moment.

The upstairs hallway was carpeted, long and narrow, with a picture window at the far end. It was wildly incongruous with everything about the inn's downstairs. A door to her right was ajar, and Pepper took that to be the place she was supposed to head.

The room's interior was reminiscent of every roadside motel Pepper had ever visited with her father in the pursuit of arcane curiosities. It fit with neither the aesthetic of the hallway nor the downstairs, but Pepper was too tired to care much. There was a full-size bed against the wall to her left, and a nightstand complete with an electric lamp. It could have felt like the most ordinary place in the world, save that it very clearly was not.

There was also an ensuite bathroom, a perfectly peculiar thing to have found in Europe regardless of present circumstances. It was tiled in green with perfectly up-to-date fixtures and a hot water tap. She took a moment to wash up, reveling in the feeling of warm water on her face and neck, and glad to have the chance to rinse out her delicates—which she hung carefully over the radiator in hopes they'd be dry by morning.

She found a blue calico nightgown folded at the foot of the bed, and happily slipped it on. It fit, and was comfortable. It was almost enough to make her less annoyed at having discovered the button on her skirt had split in half sometime during her journey.

She hung her jacket over a chair in the corner, taking a moment to sniff the still-perfect tea rose in her lapel before sliding under the covers and switching off the lamp.

She knew she would have no trouble sleeping.

Chapter 20

Pepper Jones had only ever thought she'd had a good night's sleep. But no rest in the history of her life—not in any of her travels nor in a bed she'd called her own—had she ever slept as well and as restfully as she did in the peculiar inn.

The bed was perfect: not too firm, but not too soft. The blankets were heavy enough to make her feel tucked in and secure, but not so much that they overwhelmed or overheated her. The pillow was just the right size and texture.

When Pepper's eyes came open that morning, she felt more than rested; she felt awake. She was ready to take on the task at hand. The soreness and weariness had completely evaporated from her body and her mind. Even the blisters on her feet had seemed to fade into nonexistence overnight.

Pepper made haste through her morning ablutions,

happy for the chance to brush her teeth and comb through her hair for the first time since she'd left Ardara. She got dressed quickly, careful to avoid aggravating the situation with the split metal button on her skirt waist.

Carrying her hat, purse, and jacket, Pepper headed out of the room and back down the stairs toward where she presumed she would find Vadoma and the strange woman with the bald head. Halfway down the staircase, her attention was grabbed by a clatter across the room.

A window had just blown shut. The gust of wind had blown a woman's skirt onto a stray bench nail. A man knocked over his beer trying to get to her before the skirt tore. Their child danced wildly to the happy music from the piano, oblivious to his parents' moment of difficulty.

Wait.

Wasn't that...?

Hadn't that just...? Last night...?

Pepper decided not to think too hard about it. She turned her attention toward the door between the staircase and the bar—the one the woman with the tape measure had come and gone through the previous night. The door came open just as Pepper reached the bottom step, and Vadoma emerged just enough to signal Pepper to join her on the other side of it.

The room behind the bar was dim, narrow in all dimensions, and housed a jumble of sewing, leatherworking, woodworking, and smithy tools.

But the thing that got Pepper's attention was a cage hanging near the fireplace just to her right. Within it, a man was crouched. He was unnaturally still, likely under some sort of enchantment—but at the same time wearing a look of disconcertment that Pepper found oddly contagious. She sank into a nearby chair, profoundly disturbed by what she was seeing.

"Is that what he deserves?" she asked Vadoma.

"And then some," the proprietress answered.

The woman from the night before entered then, ranting loudly in a language Pepper did not understand. She reached up to her hairline and touched the jewel that was still pinned there.

"That one's for German," Vadoma said "you would need another for Flemish. But not to bother. Your disguise is ready." She said something to the other woman then, in the language Pepper took to be Flemish from Vadoma's comment.

Pepper nodded. So that's how it worked. That would explain the numerous feathers and gems she could make out beneath Vadoma's chiffon veil. It also meant she'd need to keep hers clipped into her hair for the rest of her time in Germany. She wondered how well it would fit beneath her traveling hat.

The woman with the carved leg shook her head as she

turned and left the room. She returned moments later with a pile of black wool draped over her arms and a pair of tall, shiny boots in her hand.

"What...?" Pepper didn't manage to get her question out before the bundle of fabric was dumped into her lap. It only took her another moment to recognize what she'd been handed as a uniform—an SS officer's uniform if her memory served her. "I don't..."

Vadoma frowned and pointed toward a dressing screen in the corner of the room.

Pepper got the hint. Without bothering to finish asking her question, she stood up and stalked toward the screen, fumbling with the cumbersome uniform as she went. There was a bench behind the screen, a spindly thing with a thread-bare, greenish cushion and badly chipped paint. It sat beside a heavy iron coat rack with rust at its base.

Pepper tossed the SS officer's uniform onto the bench and began the process of unbuttoning her skirt, silently cursing the broken button as she did. Had she known she'd be changing clothes so soon, she wouldn't have bothered with fastening it up again.

Pulling on the uniform felt bizarre.

It was heavy wool, with brocade piping and insignia pinned in multiple places. There were runes embroidered on the right-hand side of the collar, and a series of dots at the corresponding place on the left. Pepper was more than a little bit creeped out by it, but she wasn't about to let that stop her from doing as she'd been instructed.

She slipped on the trousers first. The fabric wasn't as scratchy against her skin as she'd imagined it would be. And although the legs and the waist were obviously far too big for her by several inches, somehow the pants fit her perfectly as soon as she pulled them on.

Next, she tossed the white blouse over her shoulders, the too-long sleeves somehow the perfect length as her hands emerged through the cuffs. As she fastened the buttons, the garment came to a flawless fit.

The tunic was next. Careful not to disturb the pins and cords tacked all across it, Pepper slid her arms into the sleeves before fumbling through the buttons down the front. The tunic's sleeves and collar fit her as precisely and as mysteriously as the trousers and blouse had. She carefully removed the bracelet with the Labyrinth attached and tucked it into the breast pocket of the borrowed tunic. The last thing she needed was to betray her disguise with a piece of dangling jewelry—and she doubted her bracelet was an approved accessory to a Nazi uniform.

There was a warmth to the wool that reminded Pepper of being wrapped in a blanket straight off the line on a bright summer's day. Between that strange sensation and the impossible fit, Pepper was quickly coming to realize that the alterations Vadoma and the Flemish woman had done to the uniform hadn't been done solely with needle and thread.

There was power in this uniform—a strange and sickening power, but an impressive one nonetheless. She was dressed in a foreign and distasteful magic, one she hoped not to grow too comfortable within, but a magic of substance and significance. These women had clad her in some combination of the Nazis' magic and their own. Pepper wouldn't dare try and understand the depth of what had been sewn into these vestments; she figured it was enough for her to have an awareness of it all.

She'd been costumed in all the power she could possibly be gifted. She'd been loaned what magic was available for the lending. The clothes were as much armor as they were wool and silk. For the first time since considering how to cut open a salmon on her kitchen table, Pepper felt ready for whatever was about to come next.

She bent over the bench and neatly folded her own clothes upon it, careful not to crush the pink tea rose before perching on its edge to pull on the high-shined jackboots.

Stepping out from behind the screen, Pepper looked back and forth between Vadoma and the other woman. Both of them nodded distinctly as Vadoma crossed to stand before her.

"This is good," Vadoma said, reaching up and fastening a cap into Pepper's hair with a pair of wooden pins she'd been holding in the corner of her mouth. With another nod,

Vadoma took Pepper by the arm and led her over to stand before an oval-shaped mirror on the far side of the screen.

Pepper was dumbstruck by what she saw.

Her reflection had become a perfect mirror image of the man hanging above the fireplace in the cage. She couldn't help but to bring her hands up to her face as she stood agape, staring at the stranger in the looking glass.

He was a handsome man, tall and sturdy, with blue-green eyes, sandy blonde hair, and eyelashes any starlet would have paid handsomely for. But still his image turned Pepper's stomach. Wearing his face would have been unsettling enough no matter what—but having donned the mantle of an SS Lieutenant gave her a feeling of overwhelming disgust.

Vadoma had said this was good. Pepper wasn't convinced. The feeling of readiness that had girded her just a moment ago had begun to erode. She did everything she could to hang onto it while studying the stranger in the mirror.

Pepper shook her head, working to get the look of revulsion off of her borrowed face. When she couldn't stand the reflection any longer, she then looked down at unfamiliar hands, opening and closing her fists as she got used to the feeling of her new fingers.

She could hate this disguise, but she still had to make it work for her. She had to be able to use this body, to wear this uniform, and connect to its power—no matter how off-putting she found the whole arrangement.

"They will call you Pepin," Vadoma said.

"Okay," Pepper said. She jumped at the sound of her own voice. She didn't sound like herself at all. Her voice was Pepin's now, deep and resonant, with nary a hint of her usual tambour. It was at the same time unsettling and reassuring. She neither looked nor sounded like the young American woman General McCaslin had sent to stop this terrifying Nazi ritual. "Pepin," she said then, mostly to get used to the sound of this new voice. She was glad for the name—it was close enough to her own that she was unlikely to forget to answer to it.

She wondered for a moment if that's why they'd chosen the man in the cage for their kidnap victim.

"Yes. You're a Lieutenant," Vadoma answered. "You have no one who reports to you, and you are one of many who reports to your superior. You should have no trouble getting into the Castle."

"And then what?" Pepper asked. As though she didn't know. But *find this Von Sebottendorf and stop him from changing magic forever* was a little vague for her tastes, and she sincerely hoped Vadoma was going to be able to give her more information.

"You act like you belong there," she answered plainly. "You fall into rank, you find your way around the Castle. And when the time comes, you make your move."

"How will I know when the time comes?"

"You will know."

Pepper sighed. That didn't inspire confidence. Not at all.

"And how am I supposed to stop Sebottendorf from doing what he's trying to do?" she asked, then, still marveling at the sound of her own voice.

"You will know," Vadoma said again, walking around to face Pepper properly. She reached out then. Looking Pepper in the eye, Vadoma brought her fingertips to rest on the spot of the tunic directly above the pocket where she'd tucked away the Labyrinth just moments before. "You will know," she repeated slowly, a flicker of distaste curling around her mouth as though she'd just come upon something viscerally unpleasant.

Pepper understood.

It wasn't up to her to understand what she was up against. And it wasn't up to her to figure out how to defeat this man and his cult. The power in the Labyrinth would lead her.

And that was something she did understand, finally, in that moment—something she realized she should have known all along.

The Labyrinth was telling on her. It had been from the time this whole adventure began. How else had the man in the shop known for whom that fish was intended? How else would the General have known her? Or the singer? Or Vadoma and her Flemish assistant?

And how much would it tell on her in the presence of the

Nazi cult she was being sent to confront?

She still had so many questions. And she knew time was running out to get them asked.

She'd never been in a situation anything like this. All she had to compare it to was what she'd seen go on at Camp Harmony. She had no idea how many of Mr. Miyamoto's ordeals had been due to his possession of the Labyrinth. And, with the power she now understood it held within it, she was beginning to wonder not only how it would come to serve her in the battle she was about to fight, but just how badly everything might go if it fell into the wrong hands.

She had to be sure the Nazis didn't get the Labyrinth. That was one thing not in question.

Pepper wasn't completely certain as to the scope of its—or her—power. But what she did know was enough to make her certain that she absolutely had to protect it. And she knew that no one could take it from her without her permission, nor could anyone negate its healing power. That was enough to make her feel sure she could get through the ordeal she was about to embark upon.

"I can just... walk into the castle?" she asked by way of seeking reassurance.

"In that uniform," Vadoma answered, "yes."

Pepper put her hand over Vadoma's where it rested on the tunic she wore.

"What I mean is," Pepper continued, "this Sebottendorf

character is supposed to be every bit as powerful as Himmler himself. Is there any way he'll be able to detect the magic I've brought with me? Will he sense the Labyrinth? Will he know—like you knew, like General McCaslin knew, and the man in the fish shop and the woman in the café and the people in the Cabaret in Berlin..." she was rambling now, and she knew it. But she had to get this question out and asked before the time ran out and she was shooed out the door and up the mountain into a castle filled with Nazi magic.

"I don't think so," Vadoma replied softly. But Pepper could tell she wasn't sure.

"But you don't know for sure."

"I do not. Cannot," Vadoma replied. "All I can know for certain is that the cadre of soldiers with whom you will be conversing have no means of power in their possession. They are as mundane as sand. If Von Sebottendorf has made wards to protect the castle, there is a chance they will detect the presence of the Labyrinth—it houses an arcane energy far beyond their understanding, but any magic would recognize it. What we're banking on is that he and his acolytes will be counting on the wards Von Himmler cast rather than taking the time to cast their own. Sebottendorf has only arrived this morning, as Himmler was called away quite unexpectedly. It's unlikely he would insult his superior by insisting on wards of his own. But he won't be attenuated to them in the way their original caster would."

"So there's something that might detect the Labyrinth," Pepper surmised, "but it's not likely anyone up at the Castle will be able to hear the alarm even if it sounds?"

"That is a way to look at it, yes."

"And what if Sebottendorf or one of the others can see the Labyrinth like you can see it? What if he finds me out the moment we're in the same room together?"

"You will know what to do." Vadoma nodded her head then. Once. Very definitely. And then she began walking forward, taking several steps past Pepper, who could tell she'd been signaled to follow.

Pepper cringed.

There it was again: the unflinching confidence everyone she'd met on this journey had had in her ability to get this done. And once again she resolved herself to substitute their confidence for her own.

She followed Vadoma across the room and through the door.

There were a few gasps from folks who noticed Pepper in her disguise as she followed Vadoma through the main room of the inn and toward the front door. Vadoma pulled the door open and gestured for Pepper to proceed.

It was time.

Pepper froze. She stopped with her hand on the doorframe and turned back to look at Vadoma.

"And how will I get back here?" she asked. "How do I get

away? How do I get out?"

"The answer will be revealed."

Pepper frowned. That didn't inspire confidence. But, she figured, neither had much else on this journey. And it wasn't like she had much choice at the moment.

She'd agreed to this. She'd committed to this. She'd traveled far—possibly farther than she was even aware—and she'd gone so far as to put on another person's skin. She was in this now. The fate of all magic was in her hands and, escape plan or no, she was going in.

She took a deep breath and sighed, nodding to Vadoma as she reached out to pull open the heavy wooden door.

It seemed lighter. Pepper nodded to herself. That was good to know. Whatever magic it was making her body appear as that of a young SS officer was also allowing her body to function as his as well. It would take some getting used to, she figured, and she was suddenly thankful for her upcoming trek up the mountain; she could use it as a chance to take this body out for a test run. The last thing she wanted was to let these unfamiliar limbs tip off the Nazis that something was amiss.

That would just not do.

"*Auf Wiedersehn*," Pepper said to Vadoma, patting her cap where it hid the feathered jewel.

"*T'aves Baxtali*," Vadoma replied, patting Pepper on the shoulder as she turned to walk back toward the bar. Pepper had no idea what that meant, nor what language the hostess was speaking, but she decided to take the words as a kindness anyway.

She turned back to the door.

And was immediately shoved out of the way by a panting, unkempt woman barreling through it. Her face was blotched with dirt, she was dressed in rags, and her hair looked as though it hadn't been combed in weeks. The woman knocked into her hard enough that Pepper was sure, had she not been wearing a much larger and sturdier body, she'd have been bowled right over.

The strange woman seemed unaffected by the contact but stopped in her tracks as she straddled the doorway. Her mouth fell agape and she shook her head slowly.

"Pep...Pepper Jones?" she whispered in an accent as clearly Irish as any she'd heard in Adara.

Pepper started.

Who was this person? And how was it she'd been able to recognize her even though this disguise?

Was it a test?

"*Nein!*" Pepper replied. It was one of the few German expressions she was sure she could use.

The woman stumbled backward. She cried out when her back hit the door jamb, and immediately turned to run into the inn.

Pepper shrugged. That would be for Vadoma to handle.

If it wasn't safe to go, if there was a chance the people at the castle wouldn't be fooled by her disguise, she figured she'd have been warned. Whatever it was that caused the woman in the doorway to recognize her had to have been magical; she was beginning to lose count of how many times on this journey she'd been recognized by someone she'd never met before.

Pepper stepped out onto the stoop and let the door close behind her.

She placed her hand reverently over her breast pocket where the Labyrinth lay secreted. Although she'd had little opportunity to test its power, she believed in it. It had saved her life once—in a rather dramatic fashion following a direct gunshot wound to her heart at that—so she knew enough to know its power would keep her safe. What other power lay within it remained to be revealed. But even the little knowledge she had was enough. She trusted it.

And those who had called on its power trusted her.

She glanced up the path that she'd been told would lead her to Wewelsburg Castle.

It was time to go save magic.

Chapter 21

The walk up the mountain was easier than Pepper had expected it to be.

Apparently SS men were in excellent shape—or at least the one whose physique she was borrowing was. Pepin's stride was also longer, which didn't hurt things, and he had exceptionally good vision. The hard-soled, polished jackboots were more comfortable than she'd expected them to be; Pepin had apparently broken them in quite nicely before he'd been kidnapped by Vadoma and her court.

She spent the walk acclimating herself to this new body, discovering her stride and her reach, her grip strength, and just how long this body could hold its breath before the discomfort became too much.

She wound up oddly thankful when nature called. Having never had occasion to think too much about how a lad might empty his bladder, a chance to practice that particular act with no one there to bear witness was likely a very lucky happenstance. She had just enough trouble with the fly on her trousers, and with certain other necessary acts, that she was sure she'd have given something away had she needed to relieve herself for the first time in a communal Nazi washroom.

The castle loomed large on the hill up ahead, a massive, terrifying triangle punctuated by billowing red swastika flags. The spires of its two grey-capped turrets rose just a bit higher than the flat roof of the giant rotunda at the opposite end.

Pepper spent the rest of her walk dividing her attention between the path before her and the castle in the distance. She needed to inoculate herself against all she was approaching. She'd had barely a moment to study herself in a mirror, and was beginning to wish she'd taken a little time to examine how this new face expressed itself. But mostly she wondered how this new body was going to handle the heart-pounding anxiety she felt at every glance of that scarlet red Nazi flag.

She hated that flag and everything it represented. And she feared her churning guts might show themselves through her disguise and spoil everything.

Pepper remembered her mother having once said, "You'd care less about what other people think of you if you knew how seldom they actually did." She'd long taken comfort in those words, but now somehow they just rang hollow. This wasn't a bunch of schoolgirls passing judgment on her shoes or her hairstyle or what sorts of books she preferred to read—this was the Schutzstaffel, the Nazi elite, the people at the forefront of worldwide terror. And she was about to enter their most sacred space.

And she was doing it as one of them. She was sure there would be expectations, and she could only hope she would be able to meet them without compromising her ideals.

The path opened up a bit as a small guard house came into view. A gravel road merged with the foot path just a few meters before a wooden arm blocked the way of both. The arm was flanked by a wire fence that extended into the trees for a distance Pepper was unable to discern.

As Pepper approached, two men exited the guard house, one of them in a uniform matching her own, and the other dressed in the field gray of the Waffen SS. Neither of them appeared to be armed, but Pepper herself had a Walther PPK strapped to her belt, so she could be reasonably sure that these two men on sentry duty had as well.

Both men looked alarmingly like the one in the cage at the inn—like the man whose appearance she'd been lent for the occasion. Both were tall, blonde, and well-built, with gleaming insignia and polished jackboots reflecting the sun in a way Pepper found distasteful. But not as distasteful as their greeting.

"Heil Hitler!" the one in black called out to her, clicking his boot heels together.

"Heil Hitler," the other echoed.

Pepper swallowed the disgust she felt at that statement and managed to summon a smile to her face.

"Heil Hitler," she said back, thankfully sounding unaffected as she continued her approach and wondered silently if she was supposed to salute.

Pepper was glad for a moment that she'd skipped breakfast. The lurch in her guts at having heard and said those words told her a full stomach might have given her away. How long until nightfall? Pepper Jones was ready to get the work done and get the hell out of here.

But first, she had to get in.

One of the guards moved to raise the barrier, and the other cleared the path heading back into the little guard house as though nothing was even slightly irregular.

Pepper wasn't sure if it was magic at work, or some set of Nazi regulations, but she was able to pass through the checkpoint without so much as another word exchanged between herself and the two sentries.

Unable to decide whether that was good or bad, Pepper maintained her pace toward the castle.

The path inside the perimeter was steeper than it had been outside. A single uphill curve paved with stones and lined with trees led to a foot bridge over a dry moat. Pepper did her level best to look like she belonged as she made her way across the bridge and through the open arch into the castle proper.

She emerged through the archway into the castle's courtyard. Vaguely triangular in shape, it was festooned on all sides with scarlet swastika flags and silver-black banners emblazoned with the same SS Runes that Pepin's collar displayed.

The courtyard was smaller than Pepper had expected, but she supposed the group of people welcomed within the citadel's walls were likely few in number, so Himmler hadn't needed a great deal of size to accommodate them.

And what the courtyard lacked in size, it more than made up for in intensity.

There was magical energy in this place. It oozed from the stones and permeated the air with a particular arcane miasma that made the skin at Pepper's breast nearest the Labyrinth's hiding place itch as though from poison oak. Pepper had to catch her breath—she had never in her life been in the presence of such concentrated power. This whole place was like a giant focus of power—a hulking shrine to Nazi occultism.

Pepper had a limited understanding of what the Vril was, but she was sure she was soaking in it. She wondered how—and how much—the dominant energy of this place would affect her ability to do what she was here to do. What would it take to stop Von Sebottendorf? Was it even possible? And what would be the cost of trying?

Her head was swirling with questions, but there was no one to ask. All she knew—all that mattered in her estimation—was that she had to interrupt this mysterious ritual, no matter the cost. If she'd understood Mr. Miyamoto correctly, the Labyrinth had made her functionally immortal. She'd be hard to kill, maybe harder than usual while wearing this fit, sturdy body, but that didn't mean she was impervious. And it didn't mean it wouldn't hurt.

When the Labyrinth had saved her before—after she'd been shot—Pepper had been lucky that she hadn't been injured further, kidnapped, or even inspected while she was unconscious and healing. She'd felt every bit of the pain of that gunshot, too. Ability to survive notwithstanding, she would just as soon not have to contend with serious injury.

She had no magical training, no combat experience, and only the vaguest idea of why she, of all the beings who walked the earth, had been tapped for this undertaking.

But she also had no choice.

"*Pepin!*" she heard a voice call out to her from the far side of the triangular courtyard. She recognized the call had come from a stocky, golden-haired man wearing an officer's Totenkopf and rank insignia that matched her own.

"*Heil Hitler,*" Pepper presumed as she quickened her pace toward the man who'd called out to her. That seemed to be the way people greeted each other here.

"*Heil Hitler,*" the other man replied. He was holding open a door as several men in matching SS grays filed in and out, carrying sundry supply crates and bundles of firewood. "You are just in time," he said. "We've begun the preparations. Herr Sebottendorf arrived by car just an hour ago. I trust things went well with Herr Himmler?"

Pepper felt her breath catch in her throat, but was pretty sure the other man hadn't noticed the change in her.

"*Jawohl,*" she answered in her most convincing German. It occurred to her she hadn't needed to—that the gem was clearly doing its job, or else she wouldn't have understood the question. Still, there was something to be said for being genuine—particularly in a space so imbued with its own magic. There was no telling how the magic Vadoma had lent her was going to stand up in a place with so much of its own magic. She figured she ought to help it along as best she was able. "All is good," she said then, an approximate cognate to *alles gut*, a German phrase she was sure would be appropriate in this situation, and one she hoped would end all conversation concerning Heinrich Himmler.

She'd been told Himmler would be elsewhere during the ritual—a situation which had been arranged by the same beings who had arranged for Pepper's presence in the castle. But she hadn't been told why or how he'd been summoned elsewhere. And she had absolutely no idea how Pepin figured into the situation vis-à-vis the Deputy Führer.

She felt it was best to avoid the topic if at all possible.

"Excellent," the man said back, his voice sounding so American to her ears it renewed Pepper's confidence in the feathered jewel beneath her cap. "We are preparing the space."

"Already?" Pepper asked before she could stop herself. She'd wanted to avoid involved conversations with Nazis who might have known the man in the cage well enough to be sure she wasn't really him, but news of a ritual space being prepared so early in the day for a rite at sunset had surprised her enough to forget herself.

"We should have less than eight hours," the man said back, sounding less surprised at Pepper's question than she'd expected—which was good, "and Herr Von Sebottendorf will want to make an inspection. If anything is not right, we will need the time to fix it before things are to happen."

"Of course," Pepper replied.

As she'd made her way toward the castle from the inn, focused as she was on the task before her, she'd entertained the notion of corrupting the arcane space somehow as a means to sabotaging the success of the Nazi ritual. But, upon her arrival in the courtyard, the raw energy she'd sensed within the castle walls had made her question that as a potential strategy. There was too much care being taken—by both Herr Sebottendorf and the people surrounding him—to assure the space would be perfect for the rite.

She wouldn't be able to hobble the ritual. The castle's ritual space was too-well guarded and too-well prepared for anyone without magic of their own to foul. Maybe... maybe if she had a better understanding of the Labyrinth and its uses she'd be able to do what she had planned, but so far the totem had offered her only protection. She had no power of her own to wield.

She was going to have to stop Sebottendorf some other way.

Pepper watched a line of gray-clad SS men as they strode purposefully across the castle courtyard, gathered logs from a woodpile along the far wall, and bore them back across the cobblestones and through the door the man she'd just conversed with was holding open. Following their lead, Pepper scooped up a bundle of wood herself and brought it inside.

She could only hope this chore was appropriate to Pepin's rank and position. If she was doing something inappropriate or out of character, things could get very sticky very quickly. But she'd learned over the course of her life that a person could get away with a lot by acting like they knew what they were doing. She figured if she feigned confidence in this enterprise, she'd be as likely as not to get away with it.

And if these people had believed her sincere when she'd spoken the words "*Heil Hitler*," surely they'd believe her wood-hauling efforts genuine.

If she'd read the situation correctly, the firewood was headed into the ritual space. That was good. Maybe she wouldn't be able to sabotage anything, but seeing the room ahead of time—seeing the layout, figuring out an exit plan—would all be helpful; even if not in the material sense, at least it might serve to quell a bit of her anxiety.

The armful of firewood felt oddly light to Pepper as she carried it from the courtyard, through the open door, down an impressive number of stairs, and into an underground rotunda. She was mildly relieved when no one seemed to find anything irregular about her actions. Following the lead of her fellows, Pepper set to work stacking the firewood into one of the elevated fire cages ensconced on the walls of the chamber.

Pepper tried her best to appear focused on her task. She hoped the others were focused enough on theirs not to notice her level of distraction. She spent what she figured was an unsuspicious amount of time arranging each load of wood before retreating to the courtyard and returning with another. She wasn't sure how many trips she'd be allowed to make in and out of here, although the massive woodpile in the courtyard hinted that it could be as many as a dozen.

She wanted to get to know this room, to get a feeling for its particular energy. The more she understood the prepared space, the better she could brace herself for what was about to happen there.

The chamber itself was a massive affair, a giant rotunda with a recessed fire pit in the center and several windows cut into the stone to let in light from above ground. The domed ceiling was high and impressive, accounting easily for the number of stairs between this space and the ground floor. It appeared to have been cut into the mountain's natural stone and had an elaborate swastika sculpted into its apex. The room felt much more like a crypt than a chapel.

A team of officers with a ladder were at work hanging black banners and Nazi flags at intervals covering every window save the one directly opposite the door. Another team was hanging an oak wreath just above that one. And a third team was fussily draping a lectern just beneath the wreath with a red and white silk sham sporting an applique of a swastika in black velvet.

The clatter of hard-soled jackboots on the polished stone floor was deafening.

It was cold in here, too. Oddly cold. Peculiarly cold. Pepper hoped it was just the kind of thing that happened in a stone castle on a chilly day when there was no sunlight through the windows. But more likely this was an unnatural cold. Because the energy in this room was palpable.

If the castle courtyard had been overwhelming, this room's miasma was nauseating. The Labyrinth, seemingly awake for the first time since she'd left Berlin, felt hot as coal in her breast pocket; she could feel it stinging, even through the thick fabric of her borrowed uniform. She did her best to ignore it as she arranged the wood in its place.

She knew it wouldn't harm her.

The Labyrinth was the one thing keeping her from harm. Its violent reaction to the arcane energy in this room only reinforced in Pepper's mind the importance of her task. She was here to stop these madmen, and she would have to do it in this room—burning labyrinth and churning nausea be damned.

The only way in or out seemed to be the door she came in—a fact that didn't bode well for her being able to foul this ritual and get away clean. Not that getting away from a band of armed SS men while inside their sacred citadel would be a walk in the park, no matter the number and means of egress. Castles were fortresses by design, and this one had been recently reinforced by barbed wire and sentry posts—and was swarming with Nazi troopers.

Pepper was becoming increasingly convinced that she'd need to let herself be captured; let the Nazis take her out of the castle and find a way to get away after that. If she tried to escape, to find her way through this unfamiliar castle, slip through the perimeter fence and get down the mountain and back to the inn, there was every chance she'd be captured anyway; there was almost equal chance she'd be shot in the process. A bullet might not kill her, but it sure as hell would hurt. And she couldn't know for sure how well or how quickly she'd be mended by the Labyrinth's magic.

Best to avoid hot lead if she could.

If she let the Nazis capture her—if she went calmly and willingly—they would surely take her someplace and lock her up. And a locked door was one foe she could always handle. If she could get them to do the dirty work of getting her outside the castle perimeter, then she knew she'd be able to make it back to the inn.

So that would be the plan.

It wasn't a plan she liked overmuch, but it was the best plan she had. It was the first time since the strange man had handed her a wrapped fish back in Ardara that she'd felt like she was even a little bit in control of her situation. That part, she did like.

She couldn't say she felt good about things, but she felt better.

And better was something.

Chapter 22

Preparations lasted most of the day. Pepper was glad for the work. Draping fabric, hanging wreaths, and finally polishing the floor of the underground space had afforded her the time she needed to get used to the arcane energy of the place. The same way the residents of the Quay in Donegal were unaffected by the smells of low tide, Pepper had spent enough time in the castle for its intrinsic magic to begin to fade into the background.

She hadn't become completely accustomed to the buzzing and pulsing of the Nazi stronghold, but it no longer churned her guts. Even the burning of the Labyrinth against her chest had settled into a minor annoyance.

Nevertheless, Pepper took a moment to affix the Labyrinth back onto her wrist where she was accustomed to wearing it. The risk of losing her coat in the impending ordeal was far greater than the risk of losing her arm. The prospect of someone noticing it was decidedly less concerning than the idea that it could get lost.

She shoved the bracelet as far up her arm as she could, counting on a snug fit and the buttons at the cuff of her borrowed uniform to keep it out of sight. The security of having the totem in its usual place added to her feeling of readiness for whatever was coming. It didn't feel good to be in this place, but it felt just familiar enough Pepper was confident she'd be able to function with all her faculties in order.

As the sun first began its descent, dipping below the trees in the distance, the attitude among the castle's occupants shifted palpably from assiduous to anticipatory. It wouldn't be long now.

SS men in dress blacks arranged themselves into rows in the courtyard, seemingly by rank. Pepper knew little to nothing about SS rank insignia, but she knew enough about pattern matching to have that detail pegged almost immediately.

She made her way into the ranks, stationing herself between a pair of very young men whose insignia was identical to her own. The energy in the courtyard was frenetic, excitable, not at all the solemn focus she'd expect from a bunch of men about to embark upon a ritual that would change the nature of magic itself.

Pepper wondered if perhaps they didn't know.

Nazis being Nazis, she figured they'd be all in on

something like stealing the world's magic all for themselves, but she was also sure none of these troops—no doubt carefully chosen for their loyalty and blind obedience to the cult—would ever question an order from their leader. If Himmler said stand here, say this, do that, these men would do it. If Himmler told one of them to jump, he'd probably not bother asking how high; he'd just take off jumping and await further orders.

If the men in the courtyard only knew something was about to happen, but not precisely what, that could account for the almost giddy anticipation that seemed to be permeating the group.

Then again, if they did know, it could just be that none of them had any idea the difficulty or the gravity of the thing that was about to happen.

Either way, it didn't matter. All that mattered to Pepper was that she'd found her way into their ranks and no one seemed to be at all wise to her.

She knew it was possible this Sebottendorf, this powerful occultist who had come to conduct the rite in Himmler's stead, would be able to sense something was off in the room. There was a chance he'd be able to sense the presence of the Labyrinth, or the magic she was wearing along with the borrowed uniform.

She just didn't know enough about this man or his particular flavor of magic to know what he was capable of. Try as she might, she couldn't figure out that piece of the mental puzzle—save to hope that any suspicion on his part might be enough to corrupt his magic to some degree.

She would know for sure within moments.

A chant began somewhere within the castle walls and the men in the courtyard began to move. Row by row, their ranks fell into lines. They marched two abreast through the door out of the courtyard, down the pitch-dark stairway, and into the waiting glow of the rotunda.

Pepper followed along, doing her best at playing the dutiful SS officer—here to witness this great rite at the behest of Himmler, in service of the Führer himself. Those were the kinds of things she'd overheard in the courtyard as the men had begun arranging themselves into ranks.

She was surrounded by True Believers, and that was creeping her out a little bit.

The fire cages were being set alight as the SS witnesses marched in step into the rotunda, forming up in curving rows facing the lectern and oak wreath. The men fell to parade rest, and Pepper followed suit. Her toes were twitching in her boots, but outwardly showed no more signs of disquiet than any of the others.

The last of the SS witnesses had only just found their places when a fanfare sounded. Pepper's row had been near the front in the courtyard, but the ranks had reversed, leaving her in the second-to-last row. But still the trumpets behind her came as a surprise; she was proud of herself for not jumping clean out of her skin.

Her vantage point was farther from the action than she'd planned. She wasn't sure how she was going to be able to stop a ritual if she couldn't even see it.

With a second blare of trumpets, Herr Von Sebottendorf made his entrance. Sweeping in through the room's only door, a black and red cape billowing behind him, he strode through the assembled ranks as though leading a public parade.

Sebottendorf was flanked by two men dressed as ancient Teutonic knights and a dozen robed attendants. If the gossip Pepper had overheard throughout the day had been accurate, these men were Himmler's top occult deputies.

They were to become Masters of the Vril, the most powerful acolytes of the magic they were here to harness and direct. All of them were pale-skinned, tall, and had hidden their faces beneath the hoods of their robes. They kept their hands clasped in front of them and their eyes cast downward.

Pepper wasn't sure where she was supposed to look. She didn't want to miss any of the action, but at the same time didn't want to get caught gaping. After a moment, and a quick check of the men on either side of her, she settled on keeping her head down while her eyes stayed fixed on the man at the center of the rite.

Sebottendorf himself was a dumpy-looking cartoon of

a man. In any other context he might have been considered tall, but in the company of Himmler's most select Übermenschen, he appeared to be oddly short-statured. He was a stout fellow, portly almost, who hid his second chin beneath a scraggly grey goatee. He marched into the center of the room, standing just in front of the draped lectern beneath the oak wreath, looking far more like a character from a cheaply-staged opera than a skillful and capable arcane operative.

To Pepper's eyes, he didn't look at all capable of calling forth the kind of power she'd been made to understand he was planning to wield. But then again, Mr. Miyamoto hadn't looked like much, either—and she knew all too well how that had turned out.

The two men dressed in armor stood to his either side, as the twelve in robes formed a semi-circle behind the lectern. The door closed and the men in armor each took a knee. The assembled SS men came to attention all at once.

Pepper followed suit, hoping she hadn't lagged behind the others enough to call attention to herself. She kept her focus forward and did her best to keep her breathing under control.

It was time.

Whatever was going to happen here was going to happen very soon.

Sebottendorf held out his hands, palms up, as he turned his gaze toward the carved swastika in the rotunda's ceiling.

One of the men dressed in armor stood. From beneath his tabard he produced a length of white cloth. Reverently, with his eyes still cast downward, he crossed to Sebottendorf and draped the fabric across his upturned palms before returning to kneel at the occultist's side.

The other armored attendant stood then. When he brought his hands forth, he had cradled within them a small metal chest. Carved with SS runes and clasped with a swastika, the chest wore a thick green patina— making it appear centuries older than it could possibly be.

Pepper knew this kind of deception. She'd seen it time and again while working with her father. Charlatans the world over had, for time immemorial, been trying to pass off recent creations as ancient artifacts.

That the Nazis would employ such a tactic came as no surprise. They liked to portray themselves as heirs to the greatest and most ancient powers, so adding this particular humbug to their toolbox was as predictable as the sunrise. Himmler and company had set out to convince the world they were the rightful wielders of this magic—that it was ancient, and it was theirs, and that all the world should recognize their rightful place as its masters.

And with their mastery of propaganda and control of domestic media, they'd likely be able to convince a great many.

The armored man set the chest into Sebottendorf's left hand and then returned to kneel in his place.

With the kind of pomp that reminded Pepper of a High Church Catholic Mass, Sebottendorf reached his cloth-draped right hand to unfasten the clasp.

Pepper felt it the moment the seal was broken.

That metal box might be a recent creation, but the power within it was ancient.

Sebottendorf flipped back the lid, revealing a large, rough gemstone seated in a blue velvet cushion. The stone was about the size of Pepper's fist, it was purplish—an amethyst maybe—and it glinted in the firelight in a way that Pepper couldn't be sure was due to its natural facets or its powerful magic. When Holde Berge had said this stone was singularly powerful, she had not been exaggerating. Pepper's whole body tingled, and the Labyrinth pulsed against her wrist in sympathetic vibration.

Pepper wasn't sure if she'd ever been in the presence of anything like this. Even the Labyrinth had never affected her this way.

The gem thrummed in Pepper's inner ears and reverberated the stones in the room like the rumble from an angry volcano. The Labyrinth was practically singing; Pepper had to hope she was the only one who could hear it.

Her eyes darted back and forth between the stone and the occultists. If anyone else had noticed the Labyrinth's reaction, she'd do well to know as soon as possible. But the SS men's focus all remained on Sebottendorf and the proceedings at the front of the room.

Pepper turned her focus there as well.

Taking the chest in both hands, facing the gem outward toward the ranks of SS men, Sebottendorf began to mumble what was almost surely an incantation. Whatever it was, he wasn't speaking German, and Pepper had no idea what the words were, but still she knew a ritual when she saw one.

A sudden heat overtook her. Not an effect of the many pyres and the closed room, this was a blast of searing, concentrated heat that felt to Pepper like she'd just stuck her head in the oven. She did her best not to let her discomfort show on her face.

Pepper wasn't sure whether or not anyone else in the room was experiencing the magic in this way, and she didn't dare look around to check. Could all of them see the crackle, hear the thrum, and feel the heat? Or was it only the magic of the Labyrinth magnifying the power of the gem and causing her senses to react in the extreme?

Soon, she had at least part of her answer. The others in the room were experiencing something. And they weren't handling it well.

It began with the men behind Sebottendorf. Almost all at once, they lost consciousness. The dozen robed acolytes sank in slow unison onto the floor. The two men in armor weren't far behind. They each fell sideways, landing in a near-fetal position on either side of the man who was working the ritual.

Pepper had to wonder whether they were dead. She'd heard legends of powerful rites that cost human lives to work, although she wasn't necessarily sure she believed them. If such rituals existed, though, she figured something this powerful could be one. And she wouldn't put anything past Himmler—even the murder of his most elite SS troopers—if the result would mean ultimate power for himself and his Führer.

If Sebottendorf noticed the men's collapse, the onlookers couldn't tell. He gave no acknowledgement of the passed-out attendants behind and beside him, much less that he was bothered by it.

And then another man fell. Two rows in front of her and three places to her right, a soldier at attention crumpled to the floor. Moments later another one dropped, this time a man in the first row near the center.

Pepper had to wonder whether the men behind her were succumbing as well. The magic pounding in her ears drowned out sounds and turning her head to check felt like a very bad idea.

Soon there was no question left.

One after another after another the SS men fell to the floor.

Pepper shifted her gaze just enough to assure herself the man just in front of her was still breathing, placing her in a room full of unconscious men instead of a room full of dead bodies. It was a minor comfort, but she'd take whatever she could get at this point.

It wasn't long before Pepper realized she was the last person standing.

Sebottendorf, still transfixed by the gem, hadn't seemed to notice yet.

This was the moment.

This was her chance.

The magic had left her alone with Sebottendorf. His armored attendants, robed acolytes, and SS retinue were out cold and of no use to him. It was just the two of them, one-on-one.

The Occultist and the Impostor.

You will know.

That had been the answer every time she'd asked how and when and what to do to stop this ritual.

You will know.

And she did know.

Pepper leapt forward, glad for the practice she'd taken on the path to the castle. She was sure the stride of her borrowed body would easily hurdle the rows of unconscious soldiers between herself and her target.

She'd cleared half the distance between them before Sebottendorf noticed her advancing. He called out in some ancient tongue, taking his right hand from beneath the chest and flinging a ball of fire as bright and hot as the sun itself toward her. Pepper managed to dodge, but just barely. The smell of singed hair hit her nostrils, and a man on the floor cried out in pain as liquid fire hit the stones beside him and splashed onto his face and hands.

Pepper cringed at the sound, but she couldn't let herself be distracted. A slightly singed Nazi was a small price to pay for saving the world's magic from a fascist madman and his deranged disciples.

She continued her charge forward.

Sebottendorf wiggled the fingers on his still-outstretched right hand. Sparks erupted and flew in her direction, like a blast of fiery arcane buckshot. The volley was wide, and there was no way Pepper could juke to avoid it.

This was going to hurt.

With all the might she could muster from her borrowed body's toned legs, Pepper charged forward. Two more steps she ran, as hard and as fast as she could, before ducking low and diving forward toward where Sebottendorf stood.

The sparks of magic hit her like needles. Pepper gasped and groaned, squeezing her eyes shut as she hurtled forward.

By the time she caught her breath, Pepper realized she'd done what she'd aimed to do. She'd taken out Sebottendorf at his knees, knocking him backward to onto the floor. The chest had flown backward from his hands as he fell, knocking loose the still-crackling gem, which slid across the polished marble floor, coming to rest just shy of the far wall beneath the oak wreath.

Sebottendorf tossed the cloth from his left hand and moved to grapple with Pepper. His hands held her arms tight, feeling more like a pair of metal vice grips than any human grasp she'd ever felt before.

He had magic in his hands, but Pepper's borrowed body was taller, younger, and far more fit. She managed to inch herself forward, pinning Sebottendorf to the floor with her knees and bringing herself into range to punch him squarely in the face.

Her tactic worked. The punch startled him and he lessened his grip on her arms just enough for her to wriggle out of his grasp. She scrambled to her feet again, stomping Sebottendorf in the gut as she did. It hadn't been intentional, but she was glad of it. It took him a moment to catch his breath to cast again: a moment Pepper took to clamber over the pile of robed men in pursuit of her quarry.

The gem was her objective, not the occultist. And it was nearly within reach.

But Sebottendorf wasn't done. He sent a bolt of cold energy at her, hitting her in the shoulder from behind and knocking her to the ground. The wind was knocked out of her, and she didn't envy Pepin the bruises he'd develop if the magic in his uniform transferred this abuse back to him.

Pepper rolled over just in time to catch her opponent as he

dove onto her, pinning her by her shoulders with that same metallic-feeling grip she'd felt before. Sebottendorf was a big man, and the heft of his bulk was putting uncomfortable pressure on her chest. He had her by the shoulders, raging at her in various languages Pepper could only presume contained some kind of magic.

She could see the frustration on his beet-red face, hollering down at her as she struggled to free herself from his grasp. He was off-kilter, infuriated, and clearly untrained in hand-to-hand combat. Even in as much pain as she was, Pepper knew she could use this to her advantage. She summoned all her strength and threw her legs hard sideways, thankful for the leverage of her borrowed 6-plus-foot frame.

The tactic worked. Both of them rolled over, ending up with Pepper now in the superior position—pinning Sebottendorf at his waist while she moved her hands to around his throat. He still had hold of her upper arms where his grip continued to grow ever tighter and more painful. His body felt white-hot wherever she made contact. The pain in her hands was almost unbearable as she kept her grip around his throat.

Pepper channeled that pain into her grasp. The same way a child would squeeze her parent's hand to get through the pain of spreading Merthiolate on a cut, she squeezed her opponent's throat ever more tightly.

She wasn't here to kill him, but she realized in the moment

she didn't mind it if she did. Whatever happened next, she wasn't going to be the one to let go first.

He was still mumbling as she squeezed his neck, likely the incantation that was making his grip so tight.

Then he suddenly stopped. His eyes went wide and his jaw slack. His grip loosened only slightly.

Pepper felt the Labyrinth fall onto her wrist, out from under the uniform blouse and jacket where she'd taken such care to secret it. Looking down at where it had fallen, she recognized her own hand on her opponent's throat.

For whatever reason, her disguise was failing.

Any moment now, she'd be back to her normal, diminutive, feminine self and there was no way she'd be able to hold her own against a man of Sebottendorf's size. She had to get out of here immediately.

Pepper wasn't sure whether she'd done enough to keep the ritual from working. And she had to be sure. The fate of magic itself depended on her success.

With all the might she could summon from her rapidly transforming body, she lunged for the gem, leaving her startled opponent prone and growling on the floor behind her.

She didn't make it far. Sebottendorf grabbed at her leg, finding purchase at the ankle of her boot and tugging at it hard. But Pepper's frame had shrunk enough toward its natural state that the boot was too loose, coming off in his hand as she scrambled for the gem.

"*Gottverdammt!*" Sebottendorf shouted, tossing the boot to his side and moving to come to his feet.

But he was too late.

Pepper's fingers brushed the stone, sweeping it into her hand. She closed her fist around it and pulled the thing to her chest. Where Sebottendorf's flesh had felt like fire, the gem itself felt like ice. It was brutally, uncomfortably cold, but she held tight to it no less.

Pepper felt her heart slow, her breathing catch in her throat, and her limbs fail—save for the hand still clutching tight to the freezing gem. Her eyes fixed forward and she realized she couldn't see. Sounds all around her became muffled.

She could feel death closing in on her.

No mortal could safely handle that stone.

But in an instant, it passed. All of it.

She looked for a moment at the Labyrinth, where it sat on her palm just inches from where the stone was still grasped. And she knew... she knew... it had just saved her life again.

The thrum of the magic had ceased as abruptly as it had begun. Pepper's vision was flawless and her hearing was once gain crystal clear. These were her own senses, shaking off the effects of the gem and the castle.

Feeling full control of her limbs once again, Pepper shook the last of the fog out of her head and stood up straight.

Sebottendorf stumbled. Nearly to his feet, he fell to his

knees, the impact of his kneecaps on the hard stone floor making a sound that made Pepper cringe a little. He gasped for air, brought one hand to his chest and the other to his mouth, as though to try and stop himself from vomiting as the borrowed power left him.

The chill of the gem ceased all at once.

A loud crack sounded, then another.

And another.

Sudden pain, sharp and bloody, pierced Pepper's hand.

A gust of wind hit Pepper from behind, knocking the ill-fitting cap from her head, and whipping her once again feminine locks into her eyes. With her good hand, she absently brushed her hair from her face. Shards of blood-soaked amethyst fell from her loosened grip, dropping to the floor with an almost musical clatter.

Pepper turned her face to the wind, spotting as she did a new and peculiar interruption in the stone of the wall. Just beneath the oak wreath the stone shimmered and shifted—turning bright white for a moment with flecks of color and darkness swirling at its depth.

From within the swirl began to form the outline of frame and an opening door—heavy, dark, and wooden, with a knocker in the shape of a dragon's head.

She'd seen a door like this once—at the foot of the stairs leading to General McCaslin; she knew a magical exit when she saw one. She needed only to get through it.

"*Miststück!*" Sebottendorf hollered.

Pepper turned her head just far enough to see he was struggling to come to his feet. His right hand was once again outstretched in her direction. And the men in heaps on the floor were beginning to stir.

The space beyond the door didn't seem to have resolved itself fully. She wasn't sure if it was safe.

But one more glance over her shoulder was enough for her to decide she'd prefer to take her chances with a magical door than with a room full of angry Nazi occultists.

Gripping what was left of the gem in her hand, she took off toward the wall at a flat run, reaching toward the dragon's head as she charged forward.

She'd know in a moment whether that had been a good decision.

Chapter 23

Pepper wasn't looking where she was going.

She'd shut her eyes and charged forward as though there was no chance at all of a portal failure causing her to run headlong into a brick wall. A brick wall would have been infinitely preferable to what she was leaving behind her; what was a concussion in the grand scheme of saving magic, anyway?

It was almost a relief when her shin found a wooden bench in her path.

Pepper opened her eyes in time to catch herself on the edge of a nearby table. She managed to twist around as she continued falling and was able to wind up seated on the bench she'd rammed into. The final chunk of amethyst cut into her palm, but there was no way she was about to let it go now.

She looked up just in time to see General McCaslin shutting the door behind her.

As soon as the door was closed, it vanished from sight, leaving only the bare walls of the General's chamber.

She'd made it.

She was safe.

She was out of breath—burned and bruised, and wearing a stolen uniform that was missing its left boot—but she was safe.

"Here," Pepper panted, reaching out with a bloody hand to present the jagged amethyst to the General.

General McCaslin closed the space between them, taking the stone from Pepper's hand and examining it closely.

"It's broken," she whispered, her mouth falling open as her eyes narrowed. "Broken."

The General's upset was palpable. She turned to face the wall, crossing to the spot on the wall where just a moment before a door had opened and closed, bringing Pepper and that shard of amethyst back from Wewelsburg Castle. She reached her hand out, stroking the plaster with her palm, then turned her attention to studying the floor just beneath it.

Pepper had no idea what she was doing, but she knew it was uncomfortable to watch. As she turned her head to look away, she spotted—folded neatly as though they had just come from getting pressed—the traveling clothes she'd left on the bench in Vadoma's inn. She crossed to where they sat, finding beside them a basin of warm water and a towel. Beside them on the floor were her hat, gloves, shoes and handbag.

The even bigger surprise was on the table beside the basin. There, atop a crisp linen handkerchief, sat the flower Sean Michael had given her back in Ardara—still as fresh and pristine as it had been when he'd first slipped it into her buttonhole.

Pepper made quick work of getting changed. She hadn't liked wearing the Nazi uniform even when it fit. She was quite relieved to be out of it once and for all.

The broken button on her skirt had been fixed, replaced by one fashioned out of what she was pretty sure was cold iron. Pepper wasn't sure why, but she had a strong feeling it was probably for the best.

Pepper dipped the corner of the towel into the basin and did what she could to wipe the dirt from her face and blood from her already-mostly-healed hand before removing the jeweled feather clip from her hair and tucking it safely into her pocketbook. She then set to work carefully fastening the perfect pink tea rose back into her buttonhole.

The General still hadn't paid her any mind, and Pepper wasn't sure what to do next.

Should she just leave?

Were they supposed to have a conversation?

Pepper had little experience with supernatural wartime missions and she just wasn't sure what level of after-action debrief was appropriate under the circumstances.

As though sensing her confusion, the General turned to face her. There was something peculiar in her countenance as she closed the distance between herself and Pepper. Pepper couldn't place it, but something about the General had changed, and not for the better.

"The gem is broken," McCaslin said, this time addressing Pepper directly.

Pepper nodded.

"I'm not sure why it happened," she said. "It was in the fight with Sebottendorf. One minute it was whole in my hand—as smooth and as cold as a block of ice—and the next it was crumbling to shards. What I brought you is the largest piece. Or, at least, I think it's the largest."

General McCaslin held up her hand in a gesture that's universally understood as meaning "STOP".

"You broke it," she said then. Her voice was soft, but accusatory. That hadn't been a question.

"No, I didn't break it," Pepper replied. "It just crumbled in my hand."

The General's eyes flashed in a way Pepper found deeply terrifying. She would have sworn they changed color for a moment.

"You broke it," she repeated, her voice suddenly booming,

inhuman in the way it resonated. "You broke my gem!"

"I stopped the ritual," Pepper said. "I got the gem away from the Nazis and kept them from taking charge of magic as we know it!"

"What does that matter to me?" the General yelled. "You mortals and your wars and your causes," she sneered. "Six million dead here, three million there. None of that matters. None of it!"

"What are you talking about?" Pepper asked.

"This!" McCaslin replied, shoving the fractured stone in Pepper's face. Pepper stumbled backward for fear the General's hand was about to make contact. "This stone was the key to everything, you hear? Everything! This stone was formed by magic itself and guarded by Merlin for centuries. This is…" she pulled the gem back toward herself, looking down at it as she trembled with anger.

Pepper was trembling, too. She was more than a little frightened, and beginning to grow angry herself.

"You should be glad I got out with even that much," she said. "Hell," she went on, "I'm just glad I got out with my life!"

"Your life," the General spat. Pepper wasn't sure she'd ever heard so much disdain in anyone's voice as in McCaslin's at that moment. "Of what consequence is that… your life? One puny mortal in the grand scheme of things," she snarled. "I should have known you'd protect your pathetic mortal self over the sanctity of Merlin's stone."

A shadow was forming behind The General—immense, and seeming to spread from nowhere at all. Her eyes had grown unnaturally narrow, and Pepper wasn't completely sure her skin hadn't begun to change color. She shook her head and did her best not to look as terrified as she felt.

"Holde Berge said that if it got destroyed…"

"Holde Berge is scarcely less mortal than you are," The General spat. "This time her kind is in the crosshairs of history. Next time she won't care so much about who can wield this kind of power."

"If this thing matters so much to you," Pepper said, trying to let her anger take the lead over her fear. "Then why send a 'puny mortal' at all? Why not go and get the damn thing back yourself?"

"Oh if it were so easy," McCaslin replied, some of the edge leaving her voice as she once again turned her gaze to the fragment of amethyst in her hand. "I can be anywhere, at any time," she said. "But I cannot be everywhere and all at once. When a portal is opened, it is done so by magic over which I have no control. And I am unable to cross a mundane threshold." She held up the stone beside her face for Pepper to look at. "This would have changed that," she declared. "This would have allowed me to open doors on my own—to leave this space of my own volition."

"So you're a prisoner?" Pepper surmised, angrier still as the General's words sank in. "You wanted that gem so you could bust your way out and you used me to get it because none of your compatriots would bring it to you." Pepper knew her tone was disrespectful and accusatory, but she also knew she didn't care. "I stopped the Nazis from doing a terrible thing," she reminded the General. "And I'm sorry your precious rock got broken." Pepper leaned down and snagged her hat and handbag from off the floor.

"You have no idea," McCaslin growled.

Pepper, now thoroughly buttressed by fury, looked the other woman in the eye and began stepping slowly backward.

I am unable to cross a mundane threshold.

The General's words echoed in her brain. If she could just reach the door to the stairs, she'd be away from this place, and the General wouldn't be able to follow—not matter how angry she was.

"Actually," Pepper said once she was sure she was out of the General's immediate reach, "I think I understand plenty. And, you know what else?" she added, moving a little faster in hopes her hostess wouldn't be able to close the distance before she reached the exit. "I take it back. I'm not sorry at all that rock got broken. In fact, I'm only sorry I came back with any piece of it at all. I'm starting to think that maybe no one should have that much power—least of all you. Because my guess is you're locked in here for good reason. And I can only hope what's left of that stone isn't enough to do a damn thing but remind you of what you will never have."

The shadow beyond the General had grown to cover the entirety of the floor and far wall behind her. Her face had changed somehow, brow ridges becoming more pronounced, lips becoming wider, cheekbones more prominent. When her nostrils flared, Pepper was sure she saw... steam... smoke... escape from them. A guttural sound—something between the growl of a cougar and the rumble of an unstable volcano—began to fill the room.

"You were never supposed to live, Pepper Jones," The General said quietly, closing in on Pepper further as her countenance became less and less human.

There was no way to reach the door in time. Not before the dragon—and she was sure now that's what she was seeing manifest—could close the distance. And she doubted if even the Labyrinth could protect her from death by supernatural fire, much less from being eaten by a mythical creature.

On instinct, Pepper reached down to the new button on her skirt, placing her hand, and the Labyrinth, over the cold iron.

The General, the Righ, hesitated.

And that was enough.

Pepper turned on her heel and dashed the few remaining feet to the door, yanked it open, darted through to the other side, and slammed it closed behind her without so much as considering looking back.

The door shook furiously beneath her hands. The walls of

the staircase trembled along, causing trails of pebbles and dust to cascade down the uneven stones and onto the stairs. If this whole place was about to collapse in on her, Pepper was sure she'd rather be nearer the top than the bottom.

She started up the stairs at a flat run and did not stop until she could see the light from the fireplace peeking around the final bend. She was out of breath, sweating, and still quite terrified, but she was away from... whatever exactly was imprisoned below and that was going to have to be satisfactory for the time being.

She wasn't sure in that moment whether she was more angry or terrified, but what she was absolutely sure of was that she was ready to get the hell out of this place.

No one seemed to pay Pepper any mind as she slipped from the lit fireplace and back into the bustling pub above. Mostly the barroom looked the same as it had before, although there was no sign of the creepy children who had led her to the stair behind the hearth on her last visit. She made her way through the crowd quickly, anxious to be out of wherever this was and for a return to her safe little corner of the mortal world.

She'd probably be avoiding that fishmonger for a while—just to be safe.

As she moved through the jovial crowd in the pub, it was easy for Pepper to pick out several of the people who she'd helped in the General's basement the last time she'd been here. They had made themselves comfortable—smiling and talking with the folks who had been here before.

To a person, they had a drink in hand. She remembered the warnings she'd received the first time she'd come into this place. Were these people all really trapped here forever?

Pepper shook her head. She didn't want to think about what it might be like for an ordinary human to be imprisoned in this place for all eternity. That went double now that she knew there was indeed a dragon in the basement.

It was strange and horrible enough as it was—and she was only passing through.

She didn't so much as turn to look behind her as she passed out of the door and back into the street, absently rubbing the dull ache that remained in her palm and whispering a silent thanks to whomever had repaired her skirt.

At least *someone* hadn't intended for the mission to culminate in her untimely demise. Vadoma perhaps? The Flemish seamstress? She would probably never know.

What she did know, deep in her bones, that she wasn't likely to forget or forgive the supernatural beings who *had* intended for her mission to end in death. How many other people would have died in her shoes? Or ended up in an eternity of captivity? Pepper Jones believed in justice… and she swore to herself that she would never again let the supernatural world abuse human goodwill. Whatever it took.

Chapter 24

The six-hour drive between Ardara and Dublin hadn't
been anyone's idea of a good time, but all involved
agreed it had been the right move to make under the
circumstances.

After Flower had a rather protracted conversation with
Mr. Byrne the fishmonger, in which he'd been assured in the
strongest possible terms that there had been no outside help
in the shop at all this week, the trip into the capital was the
only logical next step.

The lower floors of the Dublin City Archive held a vast
library of arcane tomes, both modern and ancient. Accessible only to those with documented Talents, Horton had
expressed concern their credentials would be insufficient to
grant them admission. Flower had assured them they'd see
no difficulty.

And he had been correct.

Horton had noticed just how impressed his partner seemed at whatever credential it was their compatriot had produced in order to get them inside, but he dared not ask about it. He was having enough of a time wrapping his head around everything he'd already heard in the past few days—the last thing he was about to do was invite more chaos into his brain.

The Archive was arranged in a way that had, at first, made little sense to any of them; Horton's talent for focus and skill at navigating bureaucracy had turned out to be singularly valuable in the long and very involved process of understanding of where things were kept and how they were sorted.

"Like all things with arcane roots," he'd said to the others, examining the stacks, cabinets, and drawers for indications of what lay within, "it's chaos on the surface. But this archive, like much magic, operates on its own logic. All we need do in order to make use of these resources is to puzzle out that logic."

It had been quite a puzzle, but between them they had managed to solve it well enough.

What they'd managed to learn after a morning pouring over the Archive's relevant contents—some in volumes so old Flower had trouble reading the Old Irish calligraphy—was that they had come to the right place for more than one reason.

From their research, they'd been able to discern that an exit through the Twist was most likely to put a person back in the spot from which they'd departed: like a faerie tale that winds back to the beginning, or, as Flower had so succinctly pointed out: like a labyrinth with only one path.

Standing watch at a ferry dock wasn't anyone's idea of a good time, and there were some indications that "point of exit" didn't map exactly to geographic location in the ordinary world at all. A deeper dive into what was known and what was theorized gave them the idea that a return to Dublin was most likely, but *where* exactly wasn't necessarily discernable until it was imminent.

It was only after they'd reached this conclusion—and having listened to Cavill recount his understanding of the car chase he was quite sure had come through the Twist and back again several times—that Flower had produced an item he'd brought along from Ardara.

Cav's eyes got wide when he first caught sight of it. It was a budding tea rose, with petals so pink they looked almost unnatural.

"Is that...?" Cav asked.

"These roses grew in a bunch," he explained, gesturing with the rosebud to the place in Cavill's jacket where he kept the Compass Rose. "They're connected."

Cav pulled the Compass Rose from his pocket and carefully opened the hinge. Flower gestured for him to set the piece down on the table between open folios. As soon as Cavill's hand left the brass frame, he gently placed the tight pink bud atop the glass that held the spinning petals within.

The rosebud reacted on contact. It spun around in place and began to pulse gently, its petals slowly expanding and contracting as though it were struggling with whether or not to fully bloom.

"Yeah," Flower declared, taking hold of the Compass Rose with the animated bud still perched atop it. "I think this is going to work. Come on," he said, "let's get in the car."

Horton tried to say something about putting the books and scrolls back where they belonged, but his colleagues were out of their seats and halfway up the stairs before he could get a word out. He was still lagging behind when he reached the car. The two Americans were already in the front seat, with Flower behind the wheel and Cavill in the passenger seat with the Compass Rose and its attendant bud balanced on his right knee.

"It's gonna show us," said Flower, putting the car into gear as Horton was still situating himself in the back seat. "There's a thaumaturgic resonance to places where the world we live in has been pierced by a passage through the Twist. Knowing where it was you first lost Pepper, and knowing where the car she was in finally vanished, we have a good starting place."

He drove them out from the city center toward the river.

Horton sat forward on the seat, straining to see how the

Compass Rose and the bud atop it were behaving, but it was dark out and the streetlights weren't nearly bright enough to give him a reliable view.

"Is it working?" he asked the others.

"It's doing something," Cav said. He pointed out the driver's side window as they turned to head over the river. "That's the footbridge she crossed right before the fog showed up."

"Yeah," Flower answered, looking down at the Compass Rose as he took a hard right and then a quick left just on the other side of the river. "It's responding. We're getting what we need and then some. In fact..." Flower's eyes flew open unnaturally wide, and he slammed on the Vauxhall's brakes. "Shit," he exclaimed, "She's right there!" Flower practically jumped out of the driver's seat, leaving the car running and the headlights on. "Pepper!" he shouted.

Pepper turned her head. The voice sounded familiar, but it made no sense to her. She put her hand up to shield her eyes from the glare of the headlights as she tried to make out the figure of the man who was coming toward her.

"Pepper," he repeated, coming closer.

Pepper shook her head. It couldn't be... could it?

"Sean Michael?" she called, utterly confused and yet furiously relieved to be seeing a familiar face.

"Yeah, it's me," he said back, finally stepping close enough for her to recognize him. "Hi."

"Um... hi," Pepper said back. She was flustered, bewildered and wobbly at the knees. Her first impulse was to fling herself into his arms and demand he hold her until she stopped shaking. But something told her this was neither the time nor the place for such a display.

Sean Michael smiled at her. That helped.

"You're still wearing my flower," he said then, his voice as soothing as a toddy.

"I am." Pepper tilted her head to catch its fragrance before looking back up at Sean Michael.

"There's a lot I'm going to have to explain," he said. "But it's going to be easier now—I think."

Pepper took half a step backward and crossed her arms over her chest. She didn't like the way this conversation was going.

Two men had stepped out of the car, still stopped in the lane, and had begun walking slowly toward her. She didn't like that, either.

"What is this?" she asked pointedly. "What's going on?"

"I promise I'll explain everything," Sean Michael assured her. He reached out and placed his hand gently on her forearm.

Just then the two other men stepped into the light, and Pepper instantly recognized them from the Donegal bus station. She felt her whole body tense and wondered for a moment whether she had it in her to run.

But run to where? She certainly couldn't go back into number Twenty-A, and she surely wouldn't get much farther than that curious door before one of these three men caught up to her.

Standing her ground was going to be her only option.

"Why have you been following me?" she called to the two strangers as they approached.

"Sorry about that," Sean Michael was the one who answered. "They probably spooked you pretty bad, huh?"

Pepper nodded.

"I can assure you," Sean Michael continued, "that what my associates lack in tact, they more than make up for with good intentions. But I still don't blame you for being a little dubious."

"That's one way to put it," Pepper replied.

"Look," Sean Michael said, stepping closer to Pepper as he lowered his voice, "I really am sorry for all the cloak-and-dagger, but this is serious stuff we're dealing with."

"And we think you've gotten a taste of just how serious," Cav chimed in.

Sean Michael snapped his head around and shot Cavill a look that clearly said, 'stay out of this'. So much for pretending this was a private conversation. His hand still on Pepper's arm, he led her a few steps farther from where his partners were standing.

"What the hell is going on?" Pepper asked, loudly enough that anyone in the road would have heard her.

"Please keep your voice down," Sean Michael whispered. "Please."

"I absolutely will not," Pepper replied defiantly.

"Look," Sean Michael said, "I get it. I understand. You're kind of freaked out right now."

"You have no idea," Pepper insisted.

"Maybe I don't. But the look on your face a minute ago said that you're beginning to figure out that I know more than you think I do."

Pepper let her arms fall to her sides as she exhaled slowly. She looked Sean Michael in the eye as she nodded.

"I'll tell you everything," he said. "If you'll just get in the car," he implored, "I'll explain. I'll tell you who I am and who these guys are and what we're doing and how we know what we know. And I'll keep explaining until you don't want to hear it anymore. And if after that," he continued, "if after I've told you everything you want nothing to do with us, then I'll get lost and that will be that. But I don't think that's going to happen. I think, after you hear everything we have to say, that you're going to want to help us."

"Fat chance," Pepper replied. She'd just agreed to help a terrifying General in a basement, a cabaret singer who could split herself in two, a Romani innkeeper and her Flemish assistant, and all it had gotten her was almost killed. Whatever these men wanted with her, she was thoroughly disinclined to give. She was done being used, by anyone.

"Please," Sean Michael implored, "Please. Just get in the car. Just hear me out."

Pepper squeezed her eyes shut, pursed her lips, and held her breath. She wasn't excited about getting into a car with a couple of strangers who'd been tailing her for whatever unknown reasons. But what choice did she really have?

The fellow who'd called out to her a moment ago sounded American—and Pepper knew what that meant. They'd found her. They'd found her and they'd followed her.

And yet, they were asking her to come with them.

Something told Pepper that was a limited-time offer. If she said no now, the next time they found her, even if she could get away—which was certainly not a guarantee at this point—she doubted they'd ask her nicely again.

This might be her one chance to stop being an international fugitive. This might even be her chance to go home.

"You promise me," she said then. "All of you promise me," she added, raising her voice to a level she was sure would be audible to the two men still standing by the car, "that if I come with you now, that I hear what you have to say, when you're done I'm free to do as I choose. Promise me that I can get back out of this car and go on with my life and that all of you will leave me alone."

Horton started to answer, but Cav put a hand up to stop him.

"Yeah," Sean Michael replied. "That's tricky."

"What do you mean?"

Sean Michael sighed as he moved his hands to rest on Pepper's shoulders and looked her square in the eye.

"I don't have the power to stop anyone from looking for you," he said. "I can promise you what I won't do, what these guys won't do," he turned his head toward the two men who'd come along with him. "But I can't stop anyone else from trying to get to you. People like the man in the fishmonger's," he said, his voice slowing for added emphasis.

Pepper bristled at that. How much did Sean Michael know about what had just happened and what she'd just gone through?

"You know about that?" she asked.

"I know about a lot of things," he replied. "And I know that, if you tell us no, there's nothing I can do to stop something like that from happening again. But if you tell us yes," he added, "there are ways we can help. If you come to work with us, then you'll have a lot of people there to help you—no matter who finds you, or what it is they claim they want."

Pepper looked over at the car and then back at Sean Michael. Then she glanced back over her shoulder at the space in the wall between numbers Twenty and Twenty-One Temple Bar. These people had answers, and they were willing to share them. That was more than she could say for anyone behind that now-vanished door.

Maybe she could learn something.

Maybe she could gain some allies.

After all, she couldn't take on the entire supernatural world alone, Labyrinth or no. If these people had the resources she knew she would need, it was an opportunity she knew she couldn't miss.

"All right," she said, putting her hand out for Sean Michael to shake, "I'll come with you. As long as I have your word that I can leave whenever I care to and that none of you are going to come after me if I do."

Instead of shaking her hand, Sean Michael took it in his. He squeezed it gently then placed his other hand over the top.

"You have my word," he said.

Pepper believed him.

And, for once, she didn't blush at his touch.

EPILOGUE

1956 GROOM LAKE, NEVADA

Pepper followed her minders the way she always had, matching pace as best she could with men who were easily a foot taller. It was clear from the way she'd been greeted (if that was even the proper term) that these men weren't thrilled with a woman who had a higher clearance than they did.

If there was one thing a dozen years of doing this work had taught her, it was that the more things changed, the more they stayed the same. The haircuts were different, high-and-tight, the way only soldiers had once worn. Suits had a different cut, neckties had grown longer and more slender, patent brogues had been swapped for nubuck Oxfords; but those were only cosmetic changes. The men who wore these things were the same blindly-patriotic American zealots who had always inhabited the outer ring of US Intelligence.

Pepper found them distasteful, she always had. Blind allegiance had never been her cup of tea. But she wasn't here to deal with them. They'd be out of her sight soon enough and back to their mid-level doomsday planning.

Probably.

Whatever they were there to do, Pepper was comforted in the knowledge she was not, and would never be, one of them. Her loyalty was to herself and to humanity. No flag, no regulation, would make her behave contrary to that. She was glad for never having been asked to betray that ideal, and she could only hope that today's meeting would continue the pattern.

When President Truman had signed the order eliminating the department she'd worked for, Pepper had thought for a moment her years as a government operative were behind her. She'd been almost relieved at the thought of being released from any official obligations.

But the service had barely missed a beat before they'd been declared a necessary "black op", given a new source of funding, and an even-more-top-secret designation. In the years since, as their operations had been pushed metaphorically underground, their headquarters had been relocated literally underground.

The Groom Lake complex had been home to the Manhattan Project, a central undertaking of the American operation for the duration of the war and the years directly proceeding it. It made sense that the agency's leadership would be stationed there. But Pepper Jones, an infrequent visitor to her superior's Cold War headquarters, wasn't fond of the installation.

Unlike the charming Irish Office, the cozy, wood-paneled Arcanology Attic in Bletchley Park, or the polished brass-and-marble division post she'd first reported to in Washington D.C., Groom Lake had a sterile and almost apocalyptic quality to it.

The hallways were bare. Institutional. An endless series of white walls giving way to green linoleum floors, all lit from above by too-harsh fluorescent light and permeated by smells of artificial pine and ammonia. Even Camp Harmony had been more inviting.

Still, Pepper came when she was summoned. Because if folks in the know had decided to call on her, that meant her unique skills were necessary to a task, and that task was necessary to humanity's continued survival.

She was led into a small room that might have been an office, save for the absence of anything resembling office furniture. A small table sat in the middle of the room with gray metal chairs pulled up to it on both sides. In the one with wheels on its feet and stuffed vinyl armrests sat a man Pepper had no trouble recognizing, even though she hadn't seen him in over a decade.

Horton McDavish had grown plumper over the years. He was graying at the temples, and Pepper couldn't help but think it suited him, as did the round metal glasses he wore. He looked distinguished, if a bit old-fashioned, and oddly out of place in Groom Lake. She knew from occasional hearsay that he'd been many-times promoted and reorganized in the years since their paths had last crossed, and that he now led a much larger and more robust British Arcane Intelligence Service than had even existed during the war. As much of a surprise as it was to see him here, it was no surprise at all that he had the clearance to visit.

"Miss Jones," he greeted her, rising from his seat and extending his hand. Pepper took it, accepting his firm handshake before having a seat in the chair opposite him.

"Mr. McDavish," she said, "what a pleasant surprise."

"I hope you remain similarly disposed to my presence once we've discussed the reason I've come," he replied.

Pepper allowed her smile to fall. No time for pleasantries, then. Down to business. She set her overcoat and handbag beside her on the floor and folded her hands in her lap.

"All right," she said.

McDavish reached beneath himself to a folio Pepper hadn't noticed and pulled out a file. The thing was as thick as her arm, and displayed the British Royal Seal. Across it was stamped in red the words "TOP SECRET".

"So, what is it?" Pepper asked.

McDavish turned the file around so its contents would be readable to Pepper before flipping it open and sliding it across the desk.

"There's a situation in Ireland," he said, "and we feel like you're the person to handle it."

Pepper sighed and pulled the folder closer. The British and the Irish never had settled all their differences. It made sense for the British Service to want an American to take on this errand. And since Sean Michael's death in the Princess Victoria tragedy, Pepper Jones was the foremost American expert on Irish magic.

She looked up at McDavish and shook her head. It was only right he should be the one to send her back to Ireland for the first time since he'd first found her there. He and his partner, along with Sean Michael, had done as they'd promised that night in the Dublin street. They'd been able to tell her far more about the beings... the *creatures*... that had sent her to do their bidding in Nazi Germany; to tell her tales of the fäe that had been banished from the Earth and were still seeking a way to return. They'd told her how they'd chased her, how they'd found her, and even how they'd known where she'd been and where to find her when she came back.

And they'd told her about the Twist—a thing she was sure

she would never fully understand, but that she was glad to know was real and concrete and in some ways even predictable. It made her feel a little less bonkers.

When she'd begun to trust them enough to tell them what she'd been sent to do, not even the skeptical McDavish hinted at any disbelief. She'd been willing to go back to Bletchley Park after that, ostensibly as Mr. Weathersby's secretary from America, to render assistance as best she could.

But it was only a year later, when news was coming in about the camps in Poland and parts of Germany, that she agreed to come aboard as a full-fledged agent. The first time she'd seen the name "Birkenau" written, she'd been sick to her stomach, remembering Holde Berge's obscure warning and knowing full and well how she could have ended up there herself.

Six million people had died.

Had the Nazi ritual succeeded, it would have been billions.

She'd trammeled a genocide by an order of magnitude, but it still wasn't enough. Holde Berg had *known*. Vadoma had known. The General had known. About the camps. The atrocities. The mass graves. And they hadn't cared to interfere, or even to inform. Six million people had died because the fäe saw no value in human lives.

Pepper would never let that happen again.

She looked down at the file before her on the desk. McDavish wouldn't have come to her if this weren't serious.

"We need you to disrupt a ritual," he said.

Pepper allowed herself a wry smile.

"Going back to my roots, are we?" she half-joked.

"I don't know that it will be so difficult as all that," McDavish replied, "but if this portal is allowed to open, the consequences could be just as dire. The D.C. office has already booked your passage."

Pepper nodded once. She reached out and shut the folder, then picked it up off the table. She slid it into her handbag, sure to snap it shut before sliding it over her elbow and standing up.

"I'm on it," she told him. Pepper stepped out from behind the chair and toward the exit. She paused as she reached the doorknob. "As you may remember," she added, turning her head back to look at McDavish where he sat, "dire consequences are kind of my specialty."

THE END

ACKNOWLEDGEMENTS

There are so many people I need to thank, I'm having a hard time where to begin. So I'll start with the obvious:

Thank you to Ben Dobyns. You did all the things. From creative meetings to line edits to being excellent lunch or dinner company, this book would absolutely not exist without your incredible effort. And to everyone on the Strowlers team (with special love to Abie and Nicole!) for creating this amazing world. Thank you for being there for questions, for being (and staying) excited about the project, and for supporting me and the work even when worldwide protests and a global pandemic made everything harder for all of us. You're the kind of people an author dreams of having on her side, and I'm so lucky to have been brought into this family. I, and the book, made it through 2020 because of you and I will be forever grateful for that.

To my dear friend and muse, Lisa Coronado, for bringing Pepper into the world in a way that's so compelling I felt the immediate need to write a book about her. You're an inspiration from any angle, and it's been a joy to watch you having this adventure in my head. Thank you for your support from the very beginning, for your energy and enthusiasm, and for your readiness with answers to every burning backstory question I came at you with. You are a thousand times brilliant and I hope we get to keep telling stories together far into old age.

To the authors of Wit-n-Word: thank you for your company and for your encouragement. Being a part of a group of professionals who are as focused as they are friendly has been exceedingly helpful to me and I treasure our afternoons together—even when they have to happen over Zoom. This book would not exist without y'all.

Thank you to Elsa Sjunneson, Seanan McGuire, Laura Anne Gilman, and Jennifer Brozek for being the friends I've seen in person this year. All of you are incredible authors, wonderful people, and absolutely top-notch friends. Outdoors at a distance, or with a wave through a window, your presence in my life and in my line of sight has been a major source of joy. Thank you for sharing yourselves, and your pets, with me during these quarantimes.

To my fabulous agent, Claire Draper, thank you for navigating all things contractual and for being so encouraging, approachable, generous, and kind.

Thanks to Bria, Nanci, and the rest of the Twitter writer fam who have sprinted with me, commiserated with me, and celebrated with me long-distance. May we someday do a book tour together.

Thanks to Trish & Remy, and the Super Squad at Superhero fiction. Y'all are always there for a nudge, a cheer, or a solidarity facepalm. Your hustle is admirable, and your stories are fierce. Never change.

To Noelle Salazar, my compatriot in on-the-page Nazi fighting: may our heroines inspire us to keep kicking tail. I'm so glad we met!

To Jeremy, Dawn, Erik, Nate, and the whole Cobalt City family—you know what you did. I literally wouldn't be here without y'all.

To My President, Mary Robinette Kowal, and everyone at SFWA: thank you for putting in the work on behalf of your members (and those who aspire to become members).

And to my husband, son, and dog. Thank you for being there for me when I need you to be, and as far away as pandemic will allow when I need to concentrate. You're the best, and I wouldn't want to go through this crazy thing called life with anyone else.

And finally: to the friends, fans, and supporters of STROWLERS who found room in their hearts and their wallets to back the creation of this novel. You are powerful. Thank you for your generosity, your patience, and your incredible energy. Stories are nothing without the people we share them with. Thank you for inviting me to share this one with you.

Amanda Cherry

ABOUT THE AUTHOR

Amanda Cherry is an author/actor who still can't believe people will pay her to write books. She enjoys documentary films, fried food, and spending time on her boat. In her spare time, Amanda volunteers as an announcer and referee for Flat Track Roller Derby. She can be regularly found geeking out on Twitter @MandaTheGinger and once upon a time enjoyed appearing at SciFi/Fantasy and Comic Conventions. Amanda lives in the Seattle area with her husband, son, and the world's cutest puggle. She is represented by Claire Draper of the Bent Agency.

Find out more at www.thegingervillain.com

SHARED CINEMATIC LICENSE AGREEMENT

Strowlers isn't locked behind traditional copyright restrictions. Instead, we all play by a set of simple, shared rules. Every work is released under our Strowlers Shared Cinematic Universe License & Agreement, allowing broad rights to remix, imagine anew, and play. Do what you want with your creation, and then get excited about how others remix it into one big, collaborative story.

Strowlers Shared Cinematic Universe License & Agreement v1.0

THE PREMISES

A. The STROWLERS series of programs were first produced and put out into the Universe in 2010 by Zombie Orpheus Entertainment LLC ("ZOE").

B. ZOE created Strowlers from scratch. As creator, ZOE owns the copyrights to Strowlers and its creative elements.

C. ZOE welcomes viewers, of course. The more STROWLERS viewers, the better. Expand the community. Tell your friends.

D. ZOE, quite unusually, welcomes community members to create their own original variations, adaptations, and spin-offs of STROWLERS, provided that the new creators agree to all of the following terms.

THE TERMS

You affirm your understanding that ZOE owns the copyright to all the STROWLERS episodes that ZOE has already created or will create. That includes the stories, scripts, characters, dialogue, designs, costumes, make-up, props, cinematography, music and everything else that goes into any motion picture.

ZOE grants you a conditional, free, non-exclusive license to make and distribute your own variations, adaptations or spin-offs of STROWLERS. Really. You own the copyright to your creation, as a derivative work based on STROWLERS. This explicitly includes video, the written word, live theater, music, the visual arts, and dramatic entertainments.

BUT, "Share-Alike" applies. It's a condition of your license. You must expressly allow other folks to make free use of whatever you create for further variations, adaptations or spin-offs of STROWLERS including use of whatever new elements you create. That means that you must include or link to this license and state explicitly that your work is released under the terms of the Strowlers Shared Cinematic Universe License & Agreement. If you don't "Share-Alike," you lose your license.

"Attribution" also applies. It's a condition of your license. You have to give prominent credit to ZOE, to STROWLERS, and to the creators of any subsequent work you use to make your work. And you have to give prominent on-line links to the STROWLERS web-site and to the web-sites of any other works that you used to make your work. Crediting third-party works is by necessity a good faith effort—as more works by more creators are created using this license, it is possible that tracing originating works may become difficult. Keep an online record of the credits for your work that can updated as necessary with missing third-party credits. (The Strowlers Wiki is a good place to list your project and credited works.) If you don't give "Attribution," you lose your license.

"Transformation" counts too. It's a condition of your license. You can't just copy all or parts of STROWLERS or someone else's work. You have to create something original. In other words, we welcome you to create a transformative work, that uses but is not a mere copy of STROWLERS or someone else's work.

"Integrity" is required. It's a condition of your license. Be careful and smart when you create your work. The license from ZOE doesn't mean that all new elements you use are OK. Don't rip off anyone! For example, if you add new characters, or you add music, or you use a new story line, or you use someone else's trademarks, artworks or words in your work, be sure they are original or that you get written permission from the copyright owners of those new elements. You agree to be solely responsible for claims and damages if you don't have the integrity to do this right, and that includes indemnifying others who thereafter use any of your elements to create their own new works.

"Keep It Clean." It's a condition of your license. If ZOE perceives your derivative work to be hateful, racist, or misogynist, ZOE reserves the right to void your license and you agree that, among other remedies, ZOE can compel the immediate removal of the Strowlers name from your work or (in extreme cases) the immediate removal of the work from distribution.

"STROWLERS CANON STATUS" – If you'd like your creation to be recognized as part of the official STROWLERS Canon, you must acquire approval from ZOE's Strowlers Story Team before, during, or after you create your work. STROWLERS Canon Status will be granted at ZOE's discretion based on its Story Team's determination that your completed work fits creatively within the overall narrative of the STROWLERS universe as conceived by ZOE. Yes, this is vague—but we can't make it more specific. It's at ZOE's discretion. The advantage of receiving STROWLERS Canon Status is you can use the STROWLERS Canon logo on your work and be an official part of the story. If you generate any profits from your STROWLERS Canon work you agree to give ZOE 10% of your net profits to be used by ZOE solely to support this experiment in the creation of collective art. Your accounting and payments should be done as revenue comes in but let's face it, ZOE is not likely to sue you if you haven't paid a hundred dollars. You are becoming a member of a community and we rely upon you to do the right thing for the community. If you seem to be cheating, ZOE can at its discretion revoke your Canon Status.

"Limits on Re-use." It's a condition of your license. This license does not grant you the right to use or license any Strowlers footage, other than what is wholly original with or created by you, for broadcast television, cable television, theatrical exhibitions (except at conventions and festivals), subscription video-on-demand (SVOD) services, "over the top" delivery services (e.g. Netflix, Hulu, Amazon), without getting explicit written permission from all the copyright holders. Violation of this obligation will revoke your license and you will be responsible for any claims arising from your violation, including without limitation any claims from any entertainment industry union or guild.

Your attribution must take the following form:

Strowlers London: The Plague Years is copyright ©2018 John Doe and is released under the terms of Strowlers Shared Cinematic Universe License and Agreement:

ATTRIBUTION: This work is based on Strowlers, copyright ©2018 Zombie Orpheus Entertainment, and reuses content from Strowlers: Melbourne, copyright @2018 Jane Doe.

SHARE-ALIKE: You are free to use, remix, and transform this work in the creation of your original Strowlers stories and projects, subject to the Strowlers Shared Cinematic Universe License & Agreement

Learn more at http://scu.la/strowlers.

And, if Canon status has been approved:

STROWLERS CANON: Strowlers Pepper Jones has been approved as an official part of the Strowlers Shared Cinematic Universe story.

Printed works must also reproduce this complete license in their text.

This is an effort at a plain-English agreement but don't misunderstand. This is a contract. If you don't understand what is said, get professional advice. If you agree to all the terms and conditions set forth above, then show your acceptance by printing and emailing a signed and dated copy of this license agreement to syndication+strowlers@zombieorpheus.com.

THE STORY CONTINUES

STROWLERS EPISODES

Pilot (Seattle, USA)*
The Traveler (West Cork, Ireland)*
Amaajii (Ulaanbaatar, Mongolia)
A Small Favor (Dublin, Ireland)*
Leif and Emma (Copenhagen, Denmark)
Trudy Lane (Auckland, New Zealand)
The Labyrinth Stone (Ulaanbaatar, Mongolia)

Features Pepper Elizabeth Jones

Streaming now at
watch.thefantasy.network

and on
Amazon Prime Video

Strowlers is fan supported and creator distributed.

Sign up to help crowdfund future episodes, novels, and
other Strowlers stories at www.fan-supported.com

CPSIA information can be obtained
at www.ICGtesting.com
Printed in the USA
LVHW080100130221
679115LV00004BA/148